LITTLE VIXEN

HORSES OF

HALF MOON
RANCH

LITTLE VIXEN

JENNY OLDFIELD

Illustrated by
Paul Hunt

Hodder
Children's
Books

a division of Hodder Headline

With thanks to Bob, Karen and Katie Foster, and to the staff and guests at Lost Valley Ranch, Deckers, Colorado

First published in Great Britain in 2000
by Hodder Children's Books

The right of Jenny Oldfield to be identified as the author of
this work has been asserted by her in accordance with the
Copyright, Designs and Patents Act 1988.

10 9 8 7 6 5 4 3 2 1

A Catalogue record for this book is available from the British Library

ISBN 0 340 75730 2

Typeset by Avon Dataset Ltd, Bidford-on-Avon, Warks

Printed and bound in Great Britain by
The Guernsey Press Co. Ltd, Channel Isles

Hodder Children's Books
a division of Hodder Headline
338 Euston Road
London NW1 3BH

1

'OK, lay the lasso on the ground so Tornado can step right into it!' Sandy Scott called out the instruction to Kirstie in a calm, steady voice.

Kirstie set out the rope. The trick now was to tempt the palomino colt into this part of the arena.

Up in the saddle on Crazy Horse, one of the steadiest mounts on the ranch, Sandy held the other end of the rope and waited patiently. 'Let him take his time. It's a fine evening. We've got nothing better to do!'

'C'mon, Tornado!' Kirstie coaxed the nervous colt forward by holding on to his rope headcollar. 'The thing is, you gotta accept the saddle if you wanna train to be a good ranch horse. No bucking, no buffaloing into folks, OK?'

Tornado pulled his head back and shied away from the loop of the lasso which lay in the dust like a sleeping snake.

'Easy, boy!' Kirstie held on. No way was the spirited little palomino going to submit readily to the ritual of being backed.

Getting him to step into the noose was only the first step. After that, when the rope had tightened, there would be some kicking until Tornado realised that his companion, Crazy Horse, offered him security in this new and unnerving situation.

Then he would sidle up and walk quietly alongside Sandy and the wise old sorrel gelding, while Kirstie began the process of showing Tornado the saddle blanket, slapping it on to his back, flapping and sliding it around and gradually getting him used to the feel.

It was slow, painstaking work, but both Kirstie and her mom were in their element.

'Yeah, good!' Sandy watched the colt dance around the noose then finally step into it as Kirstie distracted him with a handful of feed. She pulled gently until it tightened around his back leg.

Feeling the slight pressure, Tornado kicked out.

Kirstie stepped quickly back. This was the part she didn't like; the colt resisting and going into flight mode, only to discover that he was tethered to Sandy and Crazy Horse. But with her mom riding the dally, she knew it would be as gentle as ever it could be, and that soon Tornado would be sidling up to the older horse, licking and chewing to show that he was ready to cooperate.

Meanwhile, she swung one leg over the fence rail and sat astride it in the evening sun, giving a wave to Ben Marsh, their head wrangler, on his way to the barn carrying bits and bridles in need of repair.

Beyond the red roof of the barn, the gentle swell of pine-covered slopes rose to the rocky horizon of Eagle's Peak, which at 12,000 feet was still sparkling white from the winter snow. Trails led there from Half-Moon Ranch, along Five Mile

Creek, through canyons, past waterfalls and up to high, crystal clear lakes. It was where Kirstie loved to be; on horseback in the mountains, riding slowly through the silver-green aspen groves or racing back along Miners' Ridge with the ranch in view in the valley below, when she would let Lucky surge into a lope and feel the wind in her hair.

'Hey, honey!' Sandy's voice broke into her dreamy thoughts. 'I said, where's that blanket? Tornado's ready!'

Sure enough; the young palomino was walking quietly alongside Crazy Horse, ignoring the halter around his leg. So Kirstie grabbed the square of heavy, striped woollen cloth from the fence and strode across the arena. She waved the blanket in front of Tornado's face, let him sniff at it, even nip it between his teeth to see if it tasted good.

'No, sorry!' she laughed, as the colt let it drop. 'This isn't for eating; this is for sliding across your shoulders and down your back, like so!'

She saw the young horse quiver and prance, then press in close to Crazy Horse. Sandy held the older gelding steady. He breathed easily, nodding his head a little as if to say, 'Easy . . . easy!'.

'See, this doesn't hurt a bit!' Kirstie soothed Tornado, flattening the blanket along his glossy golden back, trying to judge if he was ready for the next step in the backing process, which would be to fetch a saddle and rest it on top of the blanket.

But it was Sandy who made the decision that the young horse had had enough. 'He's doing great,' she told Kirstie. 'But we don't want to rush him.'

'Sure.' Taking the blanket away, she stooped to loosen the dally rope and set Tornado free.

The colt behaved like a kid let out of school. He kicked his back legs to sense the freedom, tossed his pale mane and trotted smartly to the far side of the arena.

Sandy smiled and dismounted. 'We got all the time in the world,' she said easily, tipping her white stetson on to the back of her head and letting some of her long fair hair escape.

'So we can work with him again tomorrow?' Kirstie asked eagerly. Then she laughed at herself. 'I'm rushing him, huh?'

'Yeah. And our reining champion arrives tomorrow, remember?' Leading Crazy Horse to the trough to drink, Sandy watched Kirstie fix a lead-rope on to Tornado's headcollar. 'Fresh from her success in the qualifying rounds for the national championship!'

'Great!' Kirstie was looking forward to meeting Little Vixen in the flesh. She'd seen pictures of the black-and-white paint in a copy of *American Cowboy* magazine, and when Ben Marsh had told the Scotts that he knew Vixen's rider from his days in Wyoming, the idea had developed for them to invite Brad Martin and his champion horse to Half-Moon Ranch.

'Brad could lead guests out on the trails,' Sandy had suggested. 'A celebrity wrangler! Maybe that would bring extra people in during spring.'

Kirstie's brother, Matt, had been enthusiastic. 'Yeah, we sure need the money!'

'We'd have to pay him a fee, I guess.' Ben had said he would fix a price with his old acquaintance.

Kirstie's suggestion had been the one that sealed things. 'Let's get him to give lessons. We could call it Horsemanship Week!'

'Great idea!' everyone had agreed.

That had been March. Now it was mid-May and time for Little Vixen and Brad Martin's visit.

Tomorrow, Saturday, they would welcome twenty dude guests plus the celebrity teacher and his super-gorgeous, athletic mount.

So Kirstie agreed that they might have to put off further work with Tornado.

'It's no problem. He's gonna take time, but he's a little beauty,' Sandy assured her as they released both horses in to Red Fox Meadow.

Kirstie watched the last sun's rays fall on the colt, making his coat shine golden, like a newly minted coin. Palomino was the colour of her own horse, Lucky, so she had a soft spot for little Tornado too. 'Yeah, he is,' she murmured.

'Y'know, to me this place is pretty much perfect,' Kirstie's mom sighed, leaning on the fence and watching the sun go down. 'Give me a choice between the city and the mountains, this is what I'd pick every time!'

Horses grazing the lush spring grass, a red fox stalking birds along the edge of the creek at dusk. A crimson wash overlaying the blue sky, a last glint of gold as the sun disappeared.

Sandy Scott had been brought up here in the remote valley; the daughter of cattle ranchers. She'd married and moved to live in Denver, had her children, Matt and Kirstie. But her marriage had broken up when Kirstie was ten years old and she'd brought the kids back to Half-Moon Ranch, taking it over when first Kirstie's grandpa and then her grandma had died. She'd left off the cattle ranching and turned to offering western style hospitality to paying guests; a gamble which was just beginning to pay off.

'Could you imagine living without animals . . . without all this!' Sandy spread her arms and looked up at the darkening sky.

Slowly Kirstie shook her head. 'We're lucky,' she agreed.

'. . . Very!'

Kirstie felt a glow of happiness radiate from her mom. She gazed at the horses in the ramuda, picked out her very own Lucky between Squeaky the new bay gelding and Johnny Mohawk the half-Arabian black stallion.

'And you don't regret . . . anything?' Sandy asked quietly, tinging the mood with sudden sadness.

'About you and Dad?'

Her mom nodded and gazed at the horizon.

'I guess I wish he'd keep in touch more,' Kirstie answered after a long pause. Months could go by without any word from her father. 'But I don't think we should still be all together as a family; not any more. Not really.'

This was hard for her to say, but as the years had gone by without her dad, she'd come to see that it was true.

Sandy sighed. 'We do OK, huh?'

Sliding an arm around her mom's waist, Kirstie turned her towards the ranch house. 'We do more than OK,' she insisted, marching in step over the wooden footbridge and across the gravel yard. 'We do great. We do fabulously. We do mega-mega-mega well! You'd better believe it!'

'Yee-hah!' Ben and Charlie Miller galloped ahead of the pick-up and trailer under the entrance to Half-Moon Ranch. Their horses' hooves churned up dust; their yodelling cowboy's cry drew the attention of the newly gathered guests in the yard outside the ranch house.

'Looks like Brad Martin and Little Vixen just

9

got here!' Kirstie ran inside to warn Sandy and Matt.

She leaped back down from the porch in time to see Charlie fling himself off Jitterbug and tether her to a post in the corral.

'Man, you should *see* that little darling!' the young wrangler called out. 'I took a look at her inside that trailer and I could see she was one classy lady!'

'A paint?' Kirstie recalled what she'd seen in the magazine. 'White face, black withers and hindquarters, about fourteen hands?'

'That's her!' In his excitement and rush to hold the yard gate wide open for Brad Martin's arrival, Charlie almost pushed Kirstie off-balance.

She staggered and pulled herself upright. Even Ben's thin, normally serious face was flushed and breaking out in a wide grin as he dismounted more slowly from Navaho Joe. 'Did you see her?' Kirstie demanded of the head wrangler, pushing her way through the knot of new visitors.

'Sure did.' Ben took a deep breath and punched one fist into the palm of his other hand. 'Gee, that's one mighty fine mare!'

By this time, the white pick-up was crawling

through the gate, towing its magnificent shiny trailer. The silver trim on the luxurious horse truck gleamed in the sun, its streamlined shape drawing to a slow and graceful halt.

Then the driver's door of the pick-up opened and Brad Martin stepped out. The reining expert made straight for Sandy and Matt, while Kirstie ran to the back of the trailer to help Charlie and Ben unload the horse.

'Let's lower the ramp nice and easy,' Ben advised. 'This horse is used to being trucked around the country for competition, but she won't know what to expect when we lead her out. She's gonna be wound-up, so we take it real slow!'

Easier said than done, Kirstie thought. As the ramp came down, she peered inside the air-conditioned box, eager to step inside and see the famous horse.

'OK!' Ben gave her the go-ahead to release Little Vixen from her stall.

So Kirstie went up the ramp to open the stall door, listening to the hollow stamp of the horse's hooves, hearing her shift her weight restlessly inside the cooped-up space. There was a smell of fresh straw, sweet hay and horse.

And her first view of the paint was every bit as thrilling as she'd dreamed it would be. Little Vixen's head was up, her ears fiercely pricked, nostrils flaring. She was a small-boned horse with a fine, neat head and long silky mane. The eyes were wide set and large, her body packed with muscle, making her overall shape dainty but strong.

'Wow!' Kirstie stood still in admiration for a moment. Then she unhitched the lead-rope and coaxed Little Vixen towards the ramp, proud that Ben had given her the job of introducing the

champion horse to the waiting spectators.

When they appeared together at the top of the ramp, a buzz of approval went up.

'Hey, that horse is in great shape!' someone cried out.

'She's in the Super League!'

'Whoo, that's ten thousand dollars worth of horse you're talking about!'

The murmurs went around, and no one had anything bad to say about the black-and-white paint.

Little Vixen high-stepped right on down the ramp, nodding and looking down her nose as if all this admiration was her due. *Sure, I'm a great looking horse!* she seemed to say. *I work out every day. I'm built to succeed!*

'OK, take her into the barn, bed her down,' Ben told Kirstie after Brad had checked that the horse was sound after her journey. He'd felt her knees, picked up her hooves and given her a thorough inspection.

Some visitors followed Kirstie and Vixen across the yard. 'Why doesn't she go out in the meadow?' one asked.

'Would you put a prize orchid in with a bunch

of wild columbines?' was Ben's reply.

What's wrong with columbines? Kirstie thought. Ben needn't dismiss the horses in the Half-Moon ramuda quite so easily. They had Hollywood Princess, Cadillac and Johnny Mohawk who could give most reining champions a run for their money. But she didn't really object; not with everyone so excited and honoured to have Little Vixen here.

'Open the barn door, Charlie!' Ben yelled, and the young wrangler scooted ahead to perform the task.

The wide wooden door opened on to the cool, dark space of the high-roofed barn and Kirstie led the horse inside, leaving the buzzing onlookers behind.

'This is your four diamond accommodation for the week, ma'am!' she told Little Vixen, leading her down the central aisle, with hay bales stacked to the roof on one side and a row of clean, airy stalls on the other.

In one stall they had a pregnant mare, in the next a mother and her four-day-old foal. All three came to their doors to peer out at the newcomer.

'Yeah, I know; she makes you sick!' Kirstie

acknowledged to Snowflake, the recent mother, who was a brown-and-white Appaloosa, still full-bellied after carrying her foal. 'Little Vixen has a figure to die for!'

She was smiling to herself as she came to the last stall and led the champion inside. There was hay in the net, water in the drip-feeder, a deep bed of clean straw. 'Sorry; no hot tub!' she told the pampered horse. 'But I guess we could fix that if you asked us to!'

Little Vixen walked over to her net to test out the hay. Then she rummaged in the wooden manger for grain.

'Coming up!' Kirstie ran to the nearby meal bin and brought the hungry horse a large scoop of high quality feed, satisfied to hear the teeth begin to grind and chomp. 'Is everything OK, ma'am?'

Vixen munched on without looking up.

'I take that as a yes!' Still smiling, Kirstie backed off. 'Have a nice day!' she sang as she finished her chores and ran out to join the others.

'. . . You've met Matt, and this is my daughter, Kirstie!' Sandy Scott led Brad Martin across the corral to shake hands as Kirstie emerged from the barn.

'You're kidding me!' Brad came back with a quick rejoinder. 'This ain't your daughter. This must be your sister!'

Hah-hah! How often had Kirstie heard that one? OK, so her mom looked young, but it was an old, lame joke. She stuck out her hand to have it shaken.

'And you're just as beautiful as your mom!' the visitor told her. 'Same grey eyes, same blonde hair. I bet you drive the boys wild!'

She smiled weakly and let her hand drop to her side. *No actually; they drive* me *wild . . . with boredom!*

As Brad turned his flattery back towards her mom, Kirstie ventured her first good look at him.

Brad Martin was dressed, as she would expect, in the flashy western style. His shirt was black with a white motif of horse and rider and white trim. His high-crowned hat was white, his blue jeans starched and perfectly creased. And the belt buckle was silver, personalised in gold with Brad's initials. The boots were red, black and white, and obviously custom-made.

Kirstie took all this in within seconds, as well as the guy's handsome, square features and his almost jet black hair, escaping in a wavy forelock from under the wide brim of his stetson. In the background, she also took in the disapproving frown on her brother Matt's face.

'. . . You run a great ranch!' Brad Martin told Sandy as he walked with her towards the house. 'A real neat place!'

Kirstie's mom looked relieved that the first moments had gone so smoothly; no trouble unloading the champion horse, an easily pleased celebrity guest. She led Brad on to the porch with a welcoming gesture.

Kirstie noticed that Matt was still frowning after the two of them.

'So?' he muttered when he caught her gaze.

'. . . So?' she laughed back.

'So, nothing!' he snapped, turning on his heel.

Which meant he didn't like the way their new guest was acting with their mom. Kirstie didn't have to be a genius to work that one out.

But she didn't care. Just so long as he let her take care of Little Vixen, Marlboro Man could go ahead and flirt with their mom all he liked!

2

'The key to good ridin' ain't strength,' Brad Martin insisted as he instructed a group of guests on the flat meadow by Five Mile Creek. 'It's about balance. A light touch and good balance; that's what we're talking here!'

Right on! Kirstie agreed.

'And you need to know your horse. Work out what he finds easy and what he finds hard. Then make it easy for him to do what you want him to do, and make it hard for him to go against you.'

The reining expert demonstrated the basics.

'We want Little Vixen here to move forward, OK? Now, the horse don't like the metal in her mouth being yanked, so we relax the reins. That makes it easy for her to go ahead. And she don't like my spurs digging into her sides, so she moves away from that fast as she can. Soon as she goes, I stop using my heels and she understands from two sources – her mouth and her flanks – that it's easier for her to walk on. So that's what she does!'

Little Vixen moved easily into a fluid walk which circled around the gathered group.

'You're saying you have to punish a horse to get her to do things your way?' a woman called Leah called out.

Brad rode quietly on. 'No, ma'am. Like I said: this ain't to do with strength. Take Little Vixen: see all this muscle? Why, if it came to a one to one contest over who was strongest, she could have me off her back and rollin' in the dust any time she wanted! This ain't punishment. This is asking her to do what's easiest. And the horse ain't that smart, but she's smart enough to take the easiest way; which is how come we can train a horse to do some pretty complicated stuff in the reining arena, like the flying lead changes and the 360 degree spins.'

Saying this, and without apparently doing anything that was visible to the naked eye, Brad sent Little Vixen into a perfectly executed pirouette.

Kirstie smiled at Sandy and her best friend, Lisa Goodman. This was good stuff.

'He's looks so great!' Lisa leaned out of the saddle and whispered to Kirstie.

Today's outfit was the red-and-black boots with crisp jeans and a red-and-black shirt. Brad sat upright yet easy, wearing his stirrups so long that his legs almost hung straight.

'You mean, *she* looks great!' Kirstie's attention was all on the horse.

Little Vixen had performed her dainty spin with a silky swish of her tail and mane. Her neck was arched, ears and eyes alert. And, to Kirstie, her attitude towards the workaday ranch horses was all too obvious. It said, *See that neat footwork? See that combination of strength and poise? C'mon then; show me what you guys can do!*

Enjoying the display, Kirstie leaned forward to whisper in Lucky's ear. 'We could do that!'

Lisa overheard. 'Oh sure!' she teased. 'It ain't as easy as it looks.'

'So?' Was this a challenge, Kirstie wondered.

'So, since Atlanta, reining has become an Olympic sport,' Lisa pointed out. 'It's an official discipline of the US Equestrian Team. Like, you know, dressage in England.'

'I knew that!' Kirstie was on her mettle. 'So are you saying that Lucky and me can't learn the spins and sliding stops?'

Seeing that she was hooked, Lisa grinned. 'I'm just saying it ain't as easy as it looks!'

'Which means that Kirstie will get to work on it right away,' Sandy chipped in. 'Forget backing Tornado; that's history. Ladies and gentlemen, you're looking at the prospective reining champion of Half-Moon Ranch!'

'Balance!' Kirstie reminded herself.

Lisa had set the challenge and gone on up to visit her grandpa, Lennie Goodman, at Lone Elm Trailer Park. The guests were all out on trail rides with Ben, Charlie, and the old wrangler, Hadley Crane. It was Sunday morning; exactly the right time to begin work in the arena, training Lucky in reining techniques.

'Balance ... Balance ... Whoo-oah!' Kirstie's head was spinning as she came out of a sequence of untidy spins. Lucky had got the right idea, but no way was she herself under control. In fact, she'd slid around in the deep saddle, wobbling and swaying like a beginner.

'Complicated, huh?' Brad watched from the corral with Sandy, smoke curling up from the cigarette in his hand. He threw it down, ground it with his heel and climbed the fence to give Kirstie a few tips on how to stop from getting dizzy. Then he told her to try again.

She concentrated hard, drawing the right rein against Lucky's neck and digging him in the right side with her heel to make him go into a left-hand spin. This time, she fixed her gaze on one single spot on the ground, turning like a dancer without losing her balance.

'Better!' Brad called out. He turned to Sandy. 'Your girl learns fast. I guess she takes after her mom.'

'Hey!' Sandy protested mildly. 'What makes you think I learn anything like as fast as Kirstie there?'

Brad spread his hands, palms upwards. 'Look

at this place!' he pointed out. 'You got it running like clockwork. You have the best guest cabins around this part of Colorado. The trail rides up to Eagle's Peak are great. And from what I hear tell, the owner is one pretty smart lady!'

Sandy blushed, pleased but embarrassed.

'And on top of that, you run the place single-handed!' Brad laid on the compliments with a trowel.

'Oh, no way!' This time the protest was stronger. Sandy pointed to Matt who was crossing the footbridge leading a limping Tornado. 'I couldn't do it without Matt and Kirstie. I lean on Matt to do all the financial side, and the poor kid has to combine his responsibilities here with his college studies.' Breaking away from the visitor, she went to meet her son and discuss a problem with the palomino colt.

By the time she came back, Kirstie had decided to call it a day with Lucky and was busy unsaddling him in the corral, ready to return him to the meadow.

'Tornado has a sore heel,' Sandy explained. 'No big deal. But Matt thinks he needs barn rest for a couple of days.'

Kirstie nodded. 'There's a spare stall next to Little Vixen.'

'Talking of whom ...' Brad cut in, flicking down another cigarette stub. 'It's time me and Vixen put in a little work, ready for the Gladstone Finals next month.'

So he followed Matt into the barn while Sandy lent Kirstie a hand with Lucky.

'So, what d'you think?' Sandy asked quietly, brushing Lucky down with firm, even strokes.

'Brilliant!' Kirstie enthused. 'A great athlete, excellent balance, bound to do well in the Finals!'

Her mom frowned. 'Are we talking about the same thing here?'

'The horse, of course!'

'Oh. I meant the guy. What d'you think of Brad?'

'He's OK. But, Mom, did you ever see a prettier paint than Little Vixen?' Kirstie rattled on some more, until Sandy gave up and volunteered to lead Lucky out to Red Fox Meadow.

'You stay and watch Brad and Vixen,' she advised. 'Pick up some points for you and Lucky to use.'

'Yeah, watch Brad!' Matt had come out of the

barn and sidled up alongside Kirstie as their mom walked the horse away. 'Brad-this, Brad-that! Doesn't it make you wonder what the guy's after?'

She shrugged. 'No.'

'Yeah, well . . .' Matt sniffed, drew his leather gloves out of the waistband of his jeans and put them on. 'It makes *me* ask,' he insisted, ramming the space between each finger. 'What's with the flattery? Why all the smiles and the chat?'

'Cool it, Matt.' Kirstie thought he was wound up over nothing. 'Brad's the same with everyone as far as I can tell.'

But her brother still wasn't happy. 'Nope,' he insisted, frowning at the sight of Brad Martin emerging from the barn with his horse. 'He has an eye on the main chance. Believe me, I know.'

'So?' It came down to the usual brush-off. This really didn't interest Kirstie.

'So, you like the idea of having Brad Martin around here on a permanent basis?'

'Jeez, Matt, don't you think that's a little premature?' Kirstie's brows furrowed in a small frown. 'Mom's only had a couple of short conversations with the guy!'

'Yeah, but did you see how he looks at her?'

25

'Matt!'

'OK, OK!' He backed off. 'But don't say I didn't warn you.'

Then he vanished on some other errand and Kirstie was left to ask herself if what her brother suspected might turn out to be true.

Sure, it could happen, she told herself, watching Brad mount Vixen with confident ease. Only she didn't think her mom would be ready to fall for a few shallow compliments. *She's smart. She can take care of herself*, she decided, and then concentrated hard on how exactly Brad got Little Vixen to execute the spectacular sliding stop. It was to do with the horse bracing her front legs and tucking the back ones under her, then sitting her weight backwards as the cowboy raised himself out of the saddle.

'You see these special shoes?' After the training session, Brad showed Kirstie a trick of the trade by lifting up one of Vixen's back feet.

She saw how the specially shaped horseshoe extended an inch beyond the end of the reining horse's hoof. 'It's like wearing a pair of miniature skis,' she remarked.

'Sure. I get Vixen hot-shoed by a guy in Green River, Wyoming. Costs me a hundred and fifty bucks, but you can't come close to winning a prize without them. Same with this saddle. That came to six grand, made by the finest handmade saddler in the state. But you can't cut back and buy cheap. You gotta look the part.'

Kirstie guessed that this also explained the fancy clothes and boots, not to mention the expensive white and silver trailer. 'What's the prize money like?' she asked.

Brad stood back, hands on hips. 'First prize at Gladstone in June is 100,000 dollars.'

'Wow!' Her jaw dropped.

'Yeah, but it takes a heck of a lot of work to get there.'

A phone ringing from inside the house interrupted Brad and Kirstie's talk. She ran to answer it and take a message for Brad from a man called Rex Evans.

'Martin rents an outfit from me just outside Green River. Tell him I want to speak with him; urgent!' the voice barked down the phone.

So she passed on the information and offered to take Little Vixen into the barn for Brad.

'Two scoops of feed,' he directed, quickly running off to take the call from his landlord.

When he returned five minutes later, he brought a dark cloud of bad temper into the barn with him.

'Didn't I tell you *two* scoops?' he yelled at Kirstie, striding down the central aisle.

'That's what I—' In danger of being barged to one side, she stepped aside, close to Tornado's stall.

'Not *normal* feed; Little Vixen gets special feed!' he yelled again. 'Didn't you know she needs a vitamin supplement in her grain? Jeez, I guess I have to do everything round here!'

'You didn't . . .' Kirstie began.

But it was pointless. Brad Martin's bad mood had extended to include even his precious horse. He entered the stall and pushed her into one corner, using his elbow to jab against her chest. Little Vixen's head went up in surprise, she laid her ears flat, then she retreated.

'Get some fresh straw in here,' Brad ordered, pointing accusingly at a soiled area.

Biting her lip, Kirstie did as she was told.

'Stupid horse!' she heard him say.

There was a scuffle and more barging from inside the stall. There was a grunt as Brad gave Little Vixen a second jab with his elbow.

And no thanks were offered as she reappeared with a rake and a barrow of straw, then began to muck out. Instead, Brad worked on the horse's hooves with a pick, yanking out small pebbles and pieces of grit, bullying her every time she shifted her weight. 'Stand still, for chrissake! . . . You hear me, horse? I ain't done with you yet!'

Poor Vixen endured the harsh pedicure with resignation. She hung her beautiful white head and fixed her gaze on the floor, until at last Brad was through with her.

He stood up, unhooked her bridle from its peg and flung it at Kirstie. 'Needs cleanin',' he muttered.

She caught the reins and felt the bit swing hard against her shin. *Ouch!* Only when he'd turned his back and marched out of the stall did she dare to draw breath and hop around until the pain went away.

'What got into *him*?' she grumbled quietly, listening to the rapid footsteps retreat.

Little Vixen sighed and snorted, taking two

uncertain steps to the door and casting her hurt gaze after Brad.

He didn't look back.

'We just gotta wait for him to cool off,' Kirstie decided, going up to the horse and running her hand down her neck. She too glanced towards the exit, to see Brad light up a cigarette in the doorway and stand in conversation with her mom.

'That sure is a pretty shirt,' he was telling Sandy. 'That colour blue reminds me of early morning sky way out on the plains of Wyoming.'

'Huh?' Kirstie could hardly believe it was the same man. *Talk about Dr Jekyll and Mr Hyde.*

'I'd be mighty pleased to ride out with you later today, Mrs Scott!' Brad said with jokey, old-fashioned gallantry, offering Sandy the crook of his arm.

'That was the elbow that he just used to jab you with!' Kirstie muttered to Little Vixen, who snorted again and nodded her head.

And now her mom had slipped her hand through Brad's arm and the two of them were walking across the corral together, joking and laughing.

It left Kirstie feeling uneasy as she rustled new straw into position on Vixen's bed.

'You see!' Matt sprang out of nowhere and poked his head over the stall. 'What did I tell you?'

Wearily Kirstie straightened up, listening to the laughter fade as the couple entered the house. 'Yeah, you were right!' she admitted.

For sure Brad Martin had set his sights on their mom. And now Kirstie as well as Matt was having serious doubts about the whole foolish business.

3

'Y'see this swelling under the skin here?' Matt pointed with the hoof pick to a sore patch on Tornado's heel. 'That's why he's picking the back leg up as if he has string-halt. It's like when you have a blister on your foot if your shoes are too tight; you need to take the pressure off.'

Kirstie nodded. Back from school on the Monday afternoon of Brad's Horsemanship Week, she'd quickly changed into jeans and a sweatshirt and headed out to the barn to join Matt. She liked to learn from her brother, whose veterinary course in Denver meant that he could feed a lot of useful information back to the ranch. 'What do we do now?' she asked.

'OK, we get a bucket of warm water and we throw in a couple of scoops of Epsom Salts.' Matt demonstrated as he talked. 'Then we stand the horse's hoof in the water for five minutes, and this draws out the bad stuff that's collected inside the swelling.'

Holding Tornado's head, Kirstie watched carefully. 'See, that feels good, don't it?' she soothed.

The palomino colt quietly allowed them to treat his sore foot. When the warm soaking was over, he didn't object to Matt poulticing the heel with a special wide strip of medicated lint strapped on with a tight bandage. In the end, the dressing looked neat, clean and professional.

'He stays here in the barn for a couple more days.' Matt stood back with a satisfied nod.

'And we hope he doesn't chew the dressing off!' Kirstie smiled as Tornado went into contortions, bending his neck and raising his back foot to nibble at the edge of the bandage. After a few seconds he left off and hobbled over to his manger to seek out the last few specks of grain lurking in the bottom.

'I'll put powdered bute in his next feed,' Matt decided. 'It'll help with the pain and keep down the swelling.'

'He's acting pretty well, considering.' Kirstie pointed out that not many human patients would be so tolerant.

'Sure, he's a good guy.' Patting him, Matt led Kirstie out of the stall, then took a quick look at Little Vixen next door.

The black-and-white paint appeared lonely and a little sorry for herself, head drooping over the door, eyes half closed in a bored daze.

'What's wrong? Didn't you get to work out today?' Matt inquired.

'Brad's gonna work with her in the arena after dinner. I hope to be in there with Lucky, picking up some top hints.' Kirstie was looking forward to the evening session with the reining expert.

'Hmm. I was in San Luis today. Heard a couple of things about our champion rider.' Matt dropped the remark and waited for Kirstie to pick it up.

'Yeah?'

'From what I gather, life ain't all peaches and cream for Brad Martin right now.'

'How come?' Really, Kirstie was only interested in this news if it affected Little Vixen, to whom she was happy to give some quality time before she left the barn and went in to supper.

'Cash flow problems,' Matt muttered, watching Kirstie fuss over Little Vixen. 'He owes a guy called Rex Evans thousands of dollars for the rent of the Double L outfit outside of Green River in Wyoming. I hear Brad promises and doesn't deliver. So Evans wants to move in and close him down.'

'Gee.' So this did affect the horse. Without a place to train in, Brad and Little Vixen would be in real trouble. And no wonder the rider had been in such an angry mood the morning before, after he'd taken the call from Evans. She passed this on to Matt now, and between them they agreed that the rumours were likely to be true.

It put them in thoughtful mood at the dinner table as they listened to their visitor's charm offensive on their mom.

'Great cookin',' Brad told Sandy. 'A woman

who knows how to cook steak good and rare gets my vote, yes ma'am!'

Matt cleared the plates with undisguised impatience. Cooking well and looking pretty seemed to be Brad's main criteria for judging a woman. 'Did that guy just walk off Noah's Ark?' he muttered to Kirstie as they carried the pots into the kitchen.

She grinned back and shrugged.

When they returned, Brad was midway through a tasteless tale of traditional cowboy eating. 'They do say the best way to cook a steak is to take a steer, cut off the horns, wipe its ass, show it the flame and throw it on the plate!' he laughed.

Yuck! Kirstie glanced at Sandy, relieved to see that her mom's smile was awkward and ill at ease.

Not that Brad seemed to notice. Elbows on the table, he went on to rate his own chances at the up and coming Festival of Champions in Gladstone.

'I reckon there's only Charlie Considine on Big Splash that comes anywhere close to me and Little Vixen,' he told them. 'They travel all the way up from Ocala in Florida, which gives me and Vixen an edge, because we can be there preparin' for a full week before the championship. I put a lot of hard runnin' on her during those few days to get her in really great shape.'

He paused then, as if a sudden thought had occurred. 'Hey,' he said to Sandy, 'how would you like to be my special guest? Come and see me and Vixen win the top prize up in Gladstone?'

Flattered, Kirstie's mom blushed. 'I couldn't leave Half-Moon Ranch during the summer months,' she explained. 'But thanks anyway.'

Then Sandy remembered a message she needed to pass on to Brad. 'Rex Evans called when you were out on the trail this afternoon,' she reported. 'He said Saturday was the latest he could wait, and that you'd know what it meant. Asked you to call him back.'

Matt pursed his lips and threw Kirstie a significant look.

The visitor scraped back his chair and stood up. 'Yeah, well. I got more important things in my head right now than talking on the phone. You comin', Kirstie?'

'To work with Lucky?' she checked.

'Sure. If you wanna learn the ropes on how to

become women's reining champion, there ain't no time to lose!'

'The trick is, you string the moves together smooth as silk!' Brad called to Kirstie across the arena. 'You go from a slow circle into rapid-fire fast circles, into a 360 degree spin.'

The evening training session had attracted a crowd of twenty or so spectators, including many of the week's guests, plus Sandy and Hadley.

Kirstie set Lucky into action, under Brad's eagle eye. They got through the slow, tightly woven circle, and with a touch of her heels, Kirstie moved into three fast ones, then into the spin. By the time they'd finished, her head was swimming.

'Pretty good!' Brad told her. 'But if you watch me and Little Vixen, see how we make these circles even tighter. And you have to speed up the spin!'

He worked as he spoke, demonstrating the moves perfectly so that the small crowd clapped and urged him on.

'Yee-hah, Brad!'

'Man, see that horse spin!'

'Now give us the sliding stop!'

Unable to resist the crowd-pleasing manoeuvre, Brad eased Little Vixen out towards the edge of the arena and set off at a rapid lope. The yellow dust rose from under the horse's heels as she gathered yet more pace.

'Easy, Lucky!' Kirstie murmured to her own horse, who shifted restlessly in the centre of the arena as the dust drifted into his eyes.

Brad rode Vixen on, running her hard, responding to the crowd's whoops and yells. Hat brim jammed down over his forehead, jaw set square, he got ready to rein the horse back.

But he must have forgotten that Kirstie and Lucky were still there because he cut out of the wide circle and, at full gallop, charged Vixen across the sixty foot diameter of the circle, straight into their path.

The plan was obviously to slide to a standstill before Vixen reached the far edge of the arena but, with an obstacle in his way, the champion horse had to veer to the right, throwing her rider off-balance at high speed.

There was a gasp as a frightened Lucky reared. Kirstie threw her weight forward to stay in the saddle. Grit flew into her face and she screwed her eyes tight. When she opened them again, it was in time to see Brad thrown sideways from his horse and rolling in the dust.

The crowd's yells turned to a gasp. Kirstie saw her mom and Hadley climb the fence and run; the wrangler to catch the loose horse, Sandy to help Brad to his feet.

Meanwhile, Kirstie managed to calm Lucky.

'I'm OK!' Brad was standing, his clothes covered in dirt, his hat tumbling on towards the fence. There was blood trickling from a cut on his chin and he was clutching his right shoulder.

'Call a doctor!' one of the spectators cried.

'No!' Brad pulled himself away from Sandy, insisting that the accident wasn't serious.

'But you dislocated your shoulder!' Sandy protested, seeing this from the distorted way his right arm was hanging.

By this time, Matt and Ben had come running across the corral from the barn. They climbed the fence and rushed to help Sandy cope with Brad's injury.

'If we act now, we can push the shoulder back into position, and strap the arm up,' Matt assured them after he'd taken a quick look. 'The joint

and the ligaments are pretty loose. But this is gonna hurt like hell!'

'Just do it!' Turning pale from the pain, Brad spoke through gritted teeth.

'Wait till we get in the house!' Anxious to bustle the rider somewhere private, Sandy led the way out of the arena, picking up the dusty white stetson as she went. 'You OK?' she checked with Kirstie, who nodded.

'Did someone get a hold of Little Vixen?' Brad asked and was reassured by the sight of Hadley leading the black-and-white paint quietly around the arena. He was man enough to pause alongside Kirstie and Lucky as Sandy and Matt led him gently away. 'Don't you worry your head,' he told her. 'This was down to me, one hundred per cent.'

But she felt bad about it nevertheless. It had been a shock to see Brad come off the horse. And even a minor injury could put him out of action long enough to affect his chances at Gladstone.

'Mr Big-shot!' Hadley grumbled to Ben about his Wyoming friend.

The excitement was over, the dude visitors were slowly dispersing.

'Yeah, yeah.' Ben shrugged and sighed.

'The darned fool acts like he was the Lone Ranger!' The old wrangler poured scorn on the spectacular antics in the arena. 'Hollywood cowboy!' he sniffed. 'He don't pay enough mind to his horse and, dang me, he don't even know enough to save his own skin.'

Grumble, grumble. The noises faded and the arena emptied until the only ones left were Kirstie and Lucky.

Looking up at the horizon, feeling the evening chill, she shivered. 'What now?' she whispered.

No answer from Lucky. Only a wind sweeping down from Eagle's Peak, the light fading and a new set of problems to face when they'd all had a good sleep and woken up to face a new day.

'I hope it's not true what they say: that things go wrong in threes,' Sandy Scott told Kirstie in a worried voice.

It was twenty four hours after Brad's accident; the end of a full day at school for Kirstie and plenty of time for her mom and the reining expert to have talked over his troubles. And now, early on Tuesday evening, Sandy sat on the porch swing wanting to chat.

'What happened?' Kirstie swung gently to and fro.

'Nothing yet, touch wood. But there's this big setback to Brad's chances at Gladstone; that's number one. And today, number two, he told me he's under pressure back home. He had a giant outlay on the trailer earlier this spring, which, as it turns out, has given him current problems with the rent.'

Kirstie jammed her feet on the floor to stop the swing. 'He actually told you that?'

'Yeah. We've been discussing stuff. And y'know, in spite of how Brad comes across, when you scratch beneath the surface you find quite a serious, sensitive guy.'

'Really!'

'Don't look at me like that, Kirstie. You're as bad as Matt.'

'Sorry, Mom.' She decided not to argue, but to listen and think instead.

'Sure, he's brash and ambitious. I know that. But you have to be to succeed in his world. And underneath it there's a genuinely nice human being.'

Yeah, and one with a lot to gain if he can persuade

44

Sandy Scott into sharing the profits of Half-Moon Ranch with him, Kirstie thought. Man, did she sound like her cynical older brother!

Don't jump the gun! she told herself sternly. It was still way too early to be suspecting Brad Martin of any such thing. The problem was, the idea had crept into her brain and taken root.

Then again, she thought, raising her feet to let the swing rock again. So what? If Brad really did have a genuine thing going with her mom, surely the only important thing for her and Matt was to be certain that the relationship would make Sandy happy.

'So anyway,' her mom continued, after what felt like a long, thoughtful silence. 'The best way for Brad to beat the problem with the rent—'

'Hey, Sandy! Hey, Kirstie!' Charlie Miller waved as he drove the ranch pick-up down the track in to the yard. He jumped out and carried coils of new electric wiring towards the barn, ready for the electrician to come in early next week.

'Go on!' Kirstie urged, on tenterhooks because of the interruption.

'Yeah, Brad and I are both convinced he can

solve his money problems by winning first prize at Gladstone.'

Letting out a sigh, Kirstie nodded. 'Yeah. Good thinking. But d'you reckon he really is talented enough?'

'Yes I do. And that's what he promised Rex Evans when he called him back this afternoon. Apparently, he managed to persuade him to wait another month for his dough.'

'Did Brad tell him about the current break in his preparations?' Kirstie wanted to know.

Sandy shook her head. 'No need. We had another great idea.'

Kirstie noticed how easily her mom had slipped into talking about 'we'. She frowned and shot her a quizzical glance.

'We talked it through, and Brad told me exactly what he needed to keep Little Vixen's training programme on target for Gladstone. I said I'd think about it and have a conversation with you when you got home.'

'Where do I come into it?'

'Hush and listen!' Sandy's grey eyes grew eager. 'The big thing is to keep the horse fit. And to do that we need a person who can ride real good, who knows how to handle the horse, who the horse trusts and so on . . .'

'Hey, hold on there!' Kirstie gasped. Her own eyes lit up as she predicted the rest.

But her mom took one of Kirstie's hands between hers. 'No, hear me out! Brad's seen you working with Lucky. He thinks you're a great rider; no kidding. Sure, you're only a beginner with the spins and stops, but Brad reckons Little Vixen can do those things in her sleep. She don't need a real expert; only someone to keep her working and in good shape while Brad rests up . . .'

'Whoa!' Kirstie pulled her hand away and put them both up in front of her like a traffic cop. 'You're saying Brad wants me to train Little Vixen for him?'

Breathlessly, with the same eager look, Sandy nodded. She stood up from the swing. 'Well, what d'you think? I promised Brad an answer before supper. Shall I tell him yes, Kirstie? C'mon, talk to me . . . Don't keep me in suspense!'

4

Up before dawn on Wednesday, Kirstie was out in the arena with Little Vixen before any of the guests were awake.

'Yes!' she'd said to her mom. 'Tell Brad yes!'

Never mind that she would have to get up early and work before she went to school. She didn't care that she would have no time for socialising and that she would fall exhausted into bed at the end of each day. Between now and the time when Brad Martin's dislocated shoulder healed, she, Kirstie Scott, was in charge of magnificent Little

Vixen's training programme!

'This is a chance in a lifetime!' she'd told Charlie and Matt, unable to stop talking about it all Tuesday evening.

'Little Vixen is one horse in a million!' she'd said to Hadley when she'd run up to find the old wrangler in Brown Bear Cabin to break the news.

'The horse is fine,' he'd replied. 'The problem ain't hardly ever with the horse. What you need to look at is the rider.'

'Who said there *was* a problem?' Kirstie had argued, prickling at the suggestion. Suddenly, and to her surprise, she discovered that she didn't want to hear a word said against either Little Vixen or her owner.

And Hadley had shrugged and declined to answer. 'Good luck with the horse,' he'd said grudgingly.

Undented and undaunted, she'd hardly slept for thinking about how she would work with Vixen during this first early morning session. She'd decided on flying lead changes to start with, and been glad that it would take place soon after dawn, without an audience.

'Except for me,' Brad had reminded her.

He was up and waiting for her when she came out of the house in the grey morning mist. Little Vixen was saddled and standing in the corral, ready to work.

'Lope her by the creek before you take her into the arena, get some good running on her,' Brad suggested. He was well wrapped up in a green-and-blue checked jacket, one arm of which hung empty. A bulge across the breast of the jacket showed that the right arm was held in a sling to rest the injured shoulder. Casting a cigarette butt on to the ground and stamping it out, he pointed along the mist-shrouded bank.

Kirstie nodded and sprang into the saddle. And the moment Little Vixen moved she could feel the fluid strength of the horse; the power of those muscles as she moved from walk to trot, eased her limbs, prepared to lope.

Warmed up, she went like the wind along the creek. Rabbits scuttled and bobbed down their burrows, blue jays flapped up from the bank into the dripping aspens, the very mist seemed to part with the speed of Little Vixen's gallop.

It left Kirstie breathless as she turned the horse at the start of Eden Lake Trail. But Little Vixen herself was hardly winded. She sat back slightly on her haunches, waited for the command, then shot off towards home, hooves thundering, mane flying.

'Great!' Kirstie smiled and gasped at Brad as he watched her return from the entrance to the barn. She noticed Hadley standing at the door of his cabin, looking down at them, saw her mom's bedroom light still glowing yellow through the mist. 'How about some flying lead changes in the arena?' she asked the expert.

Brad nodded his agreement, stiffening up as he saw Matt appear in the house porch. But he opened up the arena gate and told Kirstie to go right ahead.

So she wasn't paying much attention to her brother as he strode towards Brad. She was busy switching the rein from left to right, breaking up Little Vixen's rhythm to get her to lead with the opposite leg. It required precise commands and plenty of concentration, but the little black-and-white horse went beautifully, with the grace of a dancer and the strength of a world class sprinter.

'... What d'you mean, you don't want to pay me the full fee?' Brad was saying to Matt as the two men stood by the arena fence, deep in conversation.

Kirstie and Little Vixen circled the ring, so the voices rose and faded as they rode by.

'You did three days' work with the guests before the accident, so we can't pay you for the whole seven days,' Matt explained, quiet but firm. 'It figures that we'll have to refund some of the dough our guests have paid us because they're not getting a full week's tuition. Therefore we need to cut back on the fee we pay you.'

'Did you check that with your mom?' Brad sneered.

'I make the decisions about this stuff,' Matt insisted. 'And I look at the fact that you could end up costing us plenty, the way your horse eats and the fact that you asked us to provide this special feed for her. And now we can't go ahead with the horsemanship tuition, this is working out pretty expensive for the ranch.'

'Tough!' Brad turned his back and stared up over the red roof of the barn towards the mist-covered mountains. 'We had a deal.'

'So?' Matt grew more exasperated by the second. 'The deal was for seven days, not three!'

Loping round the arena, Kirstie heard and had some sympathy for both sides of the argument. Then she saw Matt and Brad move off across the corral towards the barn to continue the dispute in private.

Money! she thought with a sinking heart. She couldn't remember a time when Matt and her mom hadn't had to worry about it. There again, she knew Brad Martin was in deep trouble over his rent.

It seemed too that Little Vixen had picked up the bad atmosphere, because she slowed, faltered a couple of times and seemed less willing to work.

'OK, that's it,' Kirstie decided, pulling the horse up and leaning forward to rub her neck. 'We'll try some more stuff after I get back from school.'

She dismounted and led her out of the arena in to the corral to tether her and take off her saddle.

'. . . I'm telling you, you'll be sorry!' Brad yelled at Matt from inside the barn. 'You don't fool around with me and walk away!'

'And you don't come here to Half-Moon Ranch and push your weight around!' Matt's temper had snapped. He was shouting back. 'Maybe you fool some of the people with your smooth talking ways, but not this sucker!'

'Jeez, sonny; when you gonna grow up?' It sounded as if Brad had turned and walked away from Matt. Footsteps came towards the barn door, followed by the sound of others, then a small scuffle.

'OK, I'm not gonna punch you with your one arm hitched up in a sling like that,' Matt protested. 'But go ahead; you hit me if you wanna!'

Kirstie froze. Her heart started to thump hard as she wondered whether it would do any good for her to step in.

'Son, I wouldn't waste my energy,' Brad drawled. He swung through the door, face hidden beneath the brim of his hat. Brought up short by the sight of Kirstie, he muttered something about feed for Little Vixen, then strode off down the side of the barn.

Then Matt appeared, dishevelled and upset. He too spotted Kirstie's look of alarm. 'Don't say a word!' he warned. 'And leave Mom out of this, OK?'

She nodded nervously.

'That guy!' Matt hissed, still hardly able to contain his anger. He stepped aside as Kirstie led Little Vixen into the barn. 'He thinks he can drain us dry, but it's gonna be over my dead body!'

Kirstie felt on edge as she left for school, wishing that Matt and Brad could smooth over their differences.

The older man hadn't been seen since the argument and Matt had gone around the place with a face like a storm cloud over the Peak. Their mom had picked up the vibes and shot Kirstie a curious glance, but Kirstie had kept her word to Matt and said nothing.

So now, as she called goodbye to Sandy and came out on to the porch, there was an uncomfortable lump in her throat and a feeling that her mom had been right about bad things happening in threes: first Brad's money worries, then his accident, now the fight with Matt.

'Have a good day, honey!' Sandy called back as she always did.

Kirstie frowned. Somehow she thought not.

She slung her schoolbag over her shoulder and stepped down into the yard, where Matt was waiting to drive her up the dirt road to the intersection with Route 3 where she could wait for the school bus to pick her up.

But before she climbed into his car, something made her glance across the corral towards the barn.

The something was a whinny from Snowflake, the mother of the week old foal. At first, Kirstie assumed it was the mare calling to horses in the ramuda, reminding them that she was stuck in there until her foal was strong enough to be put out in the meadow with the others.

But Snowflake did it again, and this time the whinny was edged with definite unease. It was high and nervous, rising in volume, repeating a third and a fourth time.

'C'mon, Kirstie, move it!' Matt had started the engine. Today was a day in college for him and he was impatient to set off.

'Wait a second.' Kirstie grew determined to check up on the Appaloosa. Maybe there was something the matter with her foal.

So she dumped her bag on the car seat and ran to the barn, opening the door and stepping inside.

The first thing was the smell. Unmistakeable. It was the sweet, hot smell of smouldering hay.

The second was the curl of grey smoke winding up from the floor around a sturdy, tall pine post which supported the high roof.

Oh my God; fire!

Kirstie's thumping heart missed a beat as she gazed down the long central aisle of the wooden structure. Misty daylight filtered in at the far end, and for a moment she hoped against hope that what she was seeing wasn't smoke but creeping fog.

Then the smell invaded her nostrils in earnest and she was sure.

'Fire!' she yelled.

Snowflake kicked and barged at the door of her stall, while her tiny foal cowered in the corner and the pregnant mare next door threw back her head and whinnied high and loud.

'Fire!' Kirstie screamed.

She heard the car door slam and Matt's footsteps come running. Wrenching open the nearest door, she went in for Snickers, the pregnant sorrel mare, grabbing a headcollar and wrestling to put it around her head. The panicking mare resisted, kicking out in terror as the grey smoke curled into her nostrils.

Then Matt ran in, took in the scene and began to bring out Snowflake and the skinny, trembling foal.

It took time to persuade them out, and all the while the smoke was thickening, the smouldering hay was crackling and spurting into small red flames that began to lick up the supporting post.

Further down the aisle, Tornado and Little Vixen kicked and battered their hooves against the doors of their stalls.

Her heart in her mouth now, Kirstie pleaded with Snickers to come quickly and quietly. The smoke was pricking her eyes, making them water. And she had to hold her breath. Close behind, Matt struggled to get Snowflake and the foal to safety.

At last, they had the horses clattering and stumbling down the aisle towards the wide door.

More figures appeared; she recognised Ben and Charlie, and behind them her mom. Ben took Snickers's lead-rope from Kirstie, who raced back for Tornado and Little Vixen.

Or should she try to put out the fire?

A moment's delay could make all the difference. There was a fire extinguisher in the corner by Vixen's stall. Kirstie needed to reach it and activate the chemical spray.

'Grab Tornado!' she yelled at Matt, who was only a few feet behind her again. She was aware that he'd stepped inside the palomino's stall before a fresh pall of smoke blinded her and made her cough.

Cooler, clearer towards the floor! she told herself, dropping on to all fours to crawl past the spot where the flames were at their worst. Inside the stall, she heard Little Vixen kick desperately at the door, and above her she could see the shape of the horse's head, eyes rolling in wild terror, nostrils flared, mouth open and screaming. Acting instinctively, she reached up and unbolted the door to let the horse out into the central aisle.

Then Kirstie reached the corner and wrenched the fire extinguisher from its bracket. She directed the hose of the heavy canister at the flames, plunged the start button and saw the white foam splurge.

Before the chemical could reach the fire, a tongue of flame roared up the post behind Little

Vixen. The horse reared up on to her hind legs, front hooves pawing the air almost directly above Kirstie's head.

Kirstie staggered back, eyes streaming, throat scorching, lungs choking. The foam squirted crazily as the flames took hold.

But some instinct for survival seemed to take control of Little Vixen. Even in the thick smoke she was able to sense the best escape route, wheeling around towards the door which she couldn't now see, but probably drawn by the whinnies of the other horses and the shouts of the people arriving on the scene.

'Kirstie, where are you?' Sandy cried, battling her way into the barn.

'Stay back, Mom! Grab Little Vixen. Get her out of here!'

Above her head the flames roared and crackled. Almost blinded, she re-directed the hose and squeezed again. The foam was on target. It fought the fire, and quenched it in a billowing cloud of dark smoke.

Again! Please work! Kirstie struggled on in the stifling conditions, recognised Ben as an answer to her prayers as he loomed through the smoke

with a second extinguisher to join in the fight.

'What happened to Little Vixen?' she gasped. 'Did she make it?'

'Sandy's got her!' Ben answered. He grabbed her arm and swung her past him towards the far-off door. 'Now Kirstie, leave this to me! That's an order. You've done enough. So get out of here while you still can!'

5

A wooden structure stacked to the roof with hay and straw was a fatal combination as far as those who fought the fire were concerned.

Ben stayed inside after Kirstie staggered out, then Matt ran in to join him, armed with yet another extinguisher. He'd wrapped a wet cloth around the lower half of his face as an impromptu mask to help his breathing inside the smoke-filled barn.

But even from the yard, Kirstie could see that they were engaged in a losing battle. She saw clouds of smoke billow into the morning air, heard the crackle and crack of the flames gallop from bale to bale, up towards the metal roof.

'Thank God the horses are all out!' Sandy murmured, shaking her head in disbelief. She turned to Charlie. 'The whole barn is going up, ain't it?'

The young wrangler nodded. 'Looks that way.'

'Let's pull Matt and Ben out,' she decided, hanging her head to hide her trembling lip and tear-filled eyes.

So Charlie yelled the order for the men inside to beat a retreat. 'The boss says to save your own skins! C'mon out!'

No one answered. For a few dreadful moments the onlookers feared that smoke had overcome the brave firefighters.

Kirstie ran to the doorway. 'Matt! . . . Ben!' she cried.

Then she saw two figures stumble towards her through the dense black cloud. Behind them, orange flames licked hungrily at the tall stacks of hay. When they reached the roof, they curled and doubled back on themselves, building to a blasting inferno.

Ben emerged first into the fresh air, his face streaked with black soot and running with sweat. Then Matt appeared in a flurry of sparks. He wrenched off the improvised mask and used it to rub his stinging eyes, gasping out words of defeat.

'It's no good,' he admitted. He took in deep gulps of air. 'It's like a furnace in there. We didn't stand a chance!'

'But you're safe!' Kirstie threw both arms around her brother and drew him away from the door. 'No one got hurt!'

She looked round the yard to make sure, counting the horses – Tornado, Snickers, Snowflake, the foal, Little Vixen. Then she registered her mom, openly weeping as Hadley tried to comfort her. Charlie saw to the horses. Ben and Matt were bent double, trying to catch their breath.

Someone was missing, she realised. 'Where's Brad?' she gasped, her gaze darting back towards the blazing barn.

Hadley heard and jerked his thumb towards the slope where the cabins stood. Guests stood on the hill, roused from their beds by the noise and now mesmerized by the flames and smoke in the yard below. Amongst them, Kirstie made out the tall, dark haired figure of Brad Martin.

So everyone was accounted for. But now the danger was that the flames might reach out beyond the barn to the tack-room, and from there to the ranch house itself.

Realising there was still work to do, Hadley quickly took charge. He ordered Matt, Ben and Charlie to fetch tarpaulins, soak them in the water trough and drape them over the tack-room porch. Meanwhile, Sandy and Kirstie were joined by some of the guests. Two at a time, they darted through the barn door and dragged feed bins or whatever else they could salvage clear of the fire until the flames grew too hot and fierce for them to continue.

'OK, that's it,' Hadley told them. 'We've done all we can.'

The rest was just standing by and watching helplessly.

Flames everywhere. They roared out through the barn door and writhed into the air. Sparks flew skywards in the dense black smoke, drifted, then faded. Inside the building, the raging fire burned through beams, bringing the corrugated roof crashing down and sending a million more sparks exploding in a spectacular fountain which fell to the ground like golden rain.

So that by the time the professional firefighters arrived from San Luis, all that was left of the barn at Half-Moon Ranch was a skeleton of charred beams and a heap of smouldering remains.

Kirstie felt caved in. She sat hunched on the house porch step, watching the guys from the fire service hose down the wreckage. Dazed and trembling, she hardly took in what people said to her; only that it wasn't necessary for her to go into school that day, that she should stay home and give herself a chance to recover from the shock of the blaze.

'How are the horses?' she asked Matt for the fifth or sixth time in an hour.

'They're doing fine. Hadley took them out to the meadow. He's fixing up an electric fence to corral them and keep them separate from the rest of the ramuda until they unwind.'

'How about Snowflake's foal?'

'OK. Just a little shook up, that's all.' Matt sat down heavily on the step beside her, crooking his knees and clasping his hands around his legs. 'Like the rest of us, I guess.'

In the weary silence, Kirstie's thoughts flew to her mom. Her mind still carried a vivid picture of Sandy breaking down in tears as she realised that the flames were too strong for them to overcome. She'd hung her head, eyes closed. And when she'd looked up again, her lips had been trembling, her cheeks wet.

'Where's Mom?' she whispered to Matt.

'Down by the creek with Brad,' he said blankly.

Kirstie nodded then stood up. Scarcely aware of what she was doing, she set off across the yard, past the corral and down the side of the smouldering barn.

Smoke lingered in the air; the breeze carried small, pale grey flecks of papery ash which settled on her hair and shoulders.

Ignoring everything except her mission to find Sandy and check that she was OK, Kirstie made her way to the footbridge, where she spotted her mom and the visitor deep in conversation. But something made her stop before she reached them; maybe the isolation of the two figures and Kirstie's sense that they didn't want to be interrupted. In any case, she paused amongst the willow bushes and listened-in unobserved.

'God knows why these disasters happen,' Sandy murmured. She was leaning on a rail, staring down into the clear water. 'Just when I felt good about the ranch and hoped we could let ourselves relax a little, something like this comes along.'

'It's tough,' Brad acknowledged.

Sandy gave a small, hollow laugh. 'It's worse than tough.'

'Yeah, I know.'

'It's the *worst* thing . . . !' Clenching her fist to thud it against the rough wooden rail, Sandy tried to keep herself from breaking down again.

Brad moved in to put his arm around her shoulder and Kirstie's mom didn't resist.

'Look at it this way: when this all settles down, your insurance pays out on a new barn.' He pointed out the up side. 'You get yourselves a nice modern place instead of that creaky, leaky old one.'

'Maybe.' Sandy sighed. 'But I liked that old barn, leaky or not. My dad's dad raised the roof on it more than sixty years back.'

'I'm sorry,' Brad murmured.

'Then there's all the nonsense with the assessors. The insurance company has to send in a guy to look at the damage and give the go ahead for us to make a claim. He has to eliminate other possibilities . . .'

'Such as?' Brad cut in.

'Such as the fact that I could've started the fire myself and burned the place to the ground.' A second empty laugh followed Sandy's answer.

'No way! That's stupid!' Brad turned Sandy to face him and looked steadily into her eyes.

'We know that! But the insurance company doesn't. They deal all the time with arson cases. I guess they go around suspecting that every fire is started deliberately, so the owner can claim a pay-out and build a smart replacement.'

'But you didn't do that!' he insisted.

She frowned and shook her head. 'No. But I'm telling you it's gonna be my job to prove them wrong. You wait and see!' Throwing back her head and closing her eyes in exasperation, she slowly let herself sink forward against Brad's shoulder.

Kirstie held her breath and made sure to stay out of sight. She dropped her gaze and concentrated hard on the shallow water bubbling

70

and swirling around the smooth pebbles at the edge of the creek.

Let me not be here! she pleaded silently. *Jeez, I feel like a lousy spy!*

'It'll work out,' Brad murmured. He held Sandy close.

Kirstie swallowed hard and crouched lower. How had she got herself into this mess: hiding in the bushes from her own mother? But now she couldn't pop up like a jack-in-the-box and announce her presence. That would be too humiliating. No, now she was here, there was no way out.

'I'll do anything I can to help,' she heard Brad promise.

Then there was a muffled sigh from Sandy.

Then silence.

'Honest to God, Ben, I'm only asking a simple question!' Matt's voice was raised out in Red Fox Meadow.

It was the evening of the day of the fire. There had been trail rides as usual, guests to keep happy and horses to take care of.

But the thin curls of smoke from beneath the

doused remains of the barn served as a reminder of the disaster, together with the lingering smell of smoke in tack-room, house and cabins.

And, by the end of the day, Kirstie felt totally drained, dragging her feet as she led Jitterbug and Cadillac from the corral to the meadow.

'That ain't a simple question, and you know it!' Ben answered Matt back in the same irritable tone. He'd unfastened Yukon's headcollar and sent the brown-and-white paint off to graze.

'All I asked was, "Where was Brad when the fire happened?" ' Matt stared stubbornly at Ben, ignoring Kirstie as she too released the hardworking trail-horses into the lush green field.

'What exactly are you saying?' The head wrangler stood up to Matt in defence of his old friend.

'Nothing. I'm asking. Where was he? Why didn't he come running to get Little Vixen out of that barn? What did he do to help?'

Turning her head from one to the other, Kirstie felt like a spectator on the sidelines at a tennis match.

'That's *three* simple questions!' Ben retorted. 'You got any more?'

'Ain't that enough?' Aware that the discussion was running out of control, Matt softened. 'Listen, Ben. You know the guy better than me. Ain't his behaviour a little strange; the way he hung back instead of pitching in with us to fight the fire?'

Ben shrugged. 'He hurt his shoulder, remember.'

'Yeah, but . . .' Matt sought to express his unease in another way. 'To me, he didn't seem like he was put out none.'

'Brad don't let you know what he's thinking.' It was the way he'd always been, Ben explained. 'You gotta dig deep. But it don't mean he ain't as shocked as the rest of us.'

'Hmm.' Matt stood hands on hips, turning things over in his mind. ' "Shocked"? You put your finger on it there, Ben. I don't reckon Brad was even surprised, let alone shocked.'

Matt thinks Brad started the fire! Kirstie's sharp intake of breath made them turn.

'What?' Matt pressed her to speak out.

'Nothing . . .' She backed away. 'Really!'

But Matt persisted. He drew her in to the argument, demanding her support. 'I'm right, ain't I?'

She looked from Matt to Ben, then up the meadow at the horses quietly grazing.

'Kirstie, what do you know about this?' Matt asked, his voice low and intense.

She gazed up at the sky. 'Nothing; I swear!'

'OK, so what do you *think*?'

Sky of eggshell blue. A row of dark pine trees along the white fence. A corral at the far end of the meadow, containing Snickers, Tornado, Snowflake and her foal.

And Brad Martin's champion reining horse was there too, standing by the electric tape, head up and neck arched, alert to every movement on the darkening slopes of the Meltwater Mountains.

'I don't know what I think!' Kirstie cried at last.

She turned and ran back to the ranch, her mind a whirl of unanswered questions and her heart heavy with unspoken doubts and fears.

6

Whatever happened, life had to go on. With horses there was no let-up, even when all you wanted to do was run and hide your head until troubles went away.

So, early Thursday morning, Kirstie worked in the arena with Little Vixen on sliding stops.

'Sit back in the saddle more,' Brad advised. 'Let her ease her front legs out straight in front of her!'

His arm still in a sling, he was dressed in old jeans and worn boots, far removed from the flashy cowboy image of earlier in the week.

Practice makes perfect! Kirstie told herself. She built up Little Vixen's speed and tried the stop again. This time, the horse's back shoes slid across the dirt surface and skidded her to a spectacular halt.

'Better,' Brad grunted, turning away when he saw Matt and Charlie cross the footbridge to lead Crazy Horse and Cadillac into the corral.

Kirstie noticed Matt glare at Brad's retreating figure, then mutter to Charlie. Sighing, she reined Little Vixen away from the fence and set her into another lope around the arena. If she lost herself in the work she was doing with the horse, then she wouldn't have to think about the feud between the two men.

Likewise, at school. News of the fire at Half-Moon Ranch had got around. Questions were heaped on Kirstie's head and she told the story a dozen times.

'Who got there first?'

'Did anyone get hurt?'

'Man, I bet the horses went wild!'

She filled in the facts, left her curious audience mildly disappointed that no one had ended in hospital and that all they were left with was a boring insurance problem with the barn.

She could have described Matt's arson theory to them, but she didn't. Instead, she concentrated on the action, underplaying her own role and avoiding mentioning the ongoing bad feeling between her brother and Brad Martin.

'Gee, Kirstie, I'm sorry!' Lisa was the one who took her aside. 'This has really knocked you back, hasn't it?'

She nodded. 'I guess. But it's Mom I'm worried about. I mean, I never see her cry. But yesterday – well, yesterday hurt her bad.'

Lisa did her best to reassure her. 'It'll be OK. She'll bounce right back, believe me.'

'I hope.' Smiling gratefully, Kirstie was tempted to confess the deeper problem to her friend. But what could she say? 'I'm afraid Mom is falling in love with the guy who just set fire to our barn!'?

No way. She had to keep it to herself and hope that it did go away.

Wait and see, she told herself. *Get on with the stuff you know you can do*.

After school that day, Kirstie made a small pen

for Snowflake and her foal by roping off an area by the bank of Five Mile Creek.

'You stay in here,' she told the Appaloosa. 'Then you can feed your baby nice and quiet.'

She watched as the foal took up her suggestion and began to suckle greedily. He splayed his stick-like legs and wagged his stumpy tail as he reached out for the teat and drank his fill.

'Lucky there ain't gonna be an overnight frost,' Matt commented. 'Look on the bright side.'

He was leading Tornado across the bridge into the corral, so Kirstie followed. 'You gonna take off the bandage?' she asked.

He nodded. 'It won't stay on much longer, the way he's kicking and running around in the meadow. Anyways, he ain't holdin' back as if it's still hurtin' him, so I guess we can risk him without the dressing.'

In the corral she stood by Tornado's head while Matt busied himself with the foot, glancing at Little Vixen who was tethered nearby. 'Yeah, you next,' she promised her. 'Tonight we work some more on the spin!'

Tacked up and ready, Little Vixen snorted and stamped impatiently. *What's the hold up? Why don't we stop talkin' about it and just do it?*

'It's lookin' good,' Matt reported as he unravelled Tornado's bandage. 'No more swelling. Yeah, and it's good and clean.'

They watched as the palomino colt gingerly put the foot down on the ground. Taking weight on it didn't seem to bother him and soon he was shifting around and ignoring it completely.

'Perfect,' was Matt's verdict.

Just then, their mom leaned out of the tack-room door and beckoned them inside.

'Can't it wait?' Kirstie called. 'I need to work with Vixen before supper.'

'Is Brad there yet?' Sandy glanced to left and right. 'No. OK, you two, this will only take a second.'

So Kirstie followed Matt under the porch into the small office at the back of the tack-room.

'I just took a call from the insurers,' Sandy told them quietly. 'I thought you should know, the assessor is driving out from Denver tomorrow, Friday.'

The big day, Kirstie realised. 'What exactly will he do?'

' "She",' Sandy corrected. 'Her name's Debra

Chaney. She'll investigate the cause of the fire and assess the amount of damage.'

'But how will she find any kind of clue?' As far as Kirstie could make out, all that was left of the barn were a few uprights, a heap of charred wood and corrugated sheets scattered across the area where the barn used to be.

Sandy shrugged. 'They have their methods, I guess.'

'Think about it.' Matt spoke up. 'If someone wants to set a fire deliberately, what do they use? Maybe kerosene. This Chaney woman will be taking samples and having them tested for traces of something like that.'

'Which the lab won't find!' their mom said as firmly as she could. Nevertheless, Kirstie knew she was worried.

Matt sniffed. 'If they do, we're finished. Evidence of arson means cops, a criminal investigation, a court case . . .'

'Oh, Matt, cut it out!' Sandy pleaded. 'Why do you have to think the worst?'

'Because, what else can I do?' Matt's anxiety came across as mounting irritation. 'How does a fire start in a barn unless it was deliberate?

C'mon, tell me. I'm listenin'!'

'By accident . . .' Sandy faltered, then shook her head. She turned away and began to sift through papers on the desk.

'Accident?' Matt echoed.

'Cool it, Matt,' Kirstie whispered.

'No. I've been figurin' this out, Mom. I want you to listen.'

'Matt!' Kirstie hissed.

But Sandy turned back and met his gaze. 'OK. Go ahead.'

'Forget "accident", OK? Think "arson". Put Brad Martin right in the middle of the picture . . .'

'No!' Sandy spoke fiercely, her eyes flashing.

'Yes. Think about it. Here's a guy with money problems and a horse with a 10,000 dollar price tag. What if he suddenly thinks Little Vixen is worth more to him dead than alive?'

'You're crazy!' Sandy gasped.

'Hear me out. 10,000 dollars is what the insurance company pays out if the horse dies. Problem solved!'

'But Brad could win ten times that in prize money next month alone!' Kirstie pointed out, remembering that the regional champion had his sights firmly set on Gladstone and a national victory over Charlie Considine.

Matt shook his head. 'That's a long shot. He's up against stiff competition, and he knows it. On top of which, he's out of action because of his arm. The way he's been looking at things since Monday is that the first prize is slipping out of his grasp in double quick time.

'And Rex Evans is on his back, hassling him and threatening to throw him off the Double L. Brad's backed into a tight corner, and he has to figure a way out pretty darned fast!'

Still Sandy shook her head. Her face was pale and tense. 'I don't believe that!' she whispered.

'I haven't told you the full story yet.' With a glance at Kirstie, Matt plunged on. 'Not only does the guy stand to gain a definite pay-out of 10,000 dollars if Little Vixen dies in a fire, he also pays me back for the grudge he holds.'

'Grudge? What grudge?' Kirstie's mom was genuinely confused.

'Against me,' Matt explained. 'Look, Mom; Brad and me . . . we had a fight.'

'When was this?'

'Yesterday morning. It was over money. I said

no way could we pay him for a full week's work. He argued. It kind of got out of control.'

'What d'you mean? Why didn't I hear about this?' Sandy looked accusingly from Matt to Kirstie, who dropped her gaze. 'Did you know?'

Kirstie nodded. 'I was there.'

'For God's sake! How come I'm the last to hear?'

'Listen, Mom, that ain't the point. Brad built up this grudge. He yells at me and tells me I'll be sorry.'

'Is that true?' Sandy asked Kirstie.

'Yes,' she answered quietly. She could hear the blood rushing through her veins as her head began to throb with tension.

'He tells me I'll regret messing him around. An hour later, the barn goes up in smoke!'

Sandy's eyes widened as she swung round to confront her son. 'This is nonsense, Matt. The problem is, you're jealous of Brad! That's why you've made up this ridiculous story. You can't stand to have the guy around!'

'Oh, sure!' Matt scoffed.

'It's true. Just because Brad comes across with the flattery, you decide his motives are all wrong.

Sure, it's shallow, cheap stuff and no way am I taken in by it. But I like the guy anyway. I don't have to justify that to you.' Sandy's voice dropped to a whisper and once again she was on the point of tears.

During the silence, Matt battled with his own emotions. He went back to the old question. 'So where was Brad when the fire started?'

It made Sandy gasp in despair and turn back to Kirstie.

'Don't put me in the middle here!' Kirstie begged, pulled this way and that by the arguments she'd heard.

She went to the door of the tack-room and stared out at Little Vixen tethered to the post. She remembered the fear in the horse's eyes as the flames had leaped up; the wild eyes, the bunched up terror.

Brad wouldn't . . .!

Behind her, Sandy broke down and began to sob, rejecting Matt's remorseful attempt to comfort her.

'Go away!' she cried, bundling him out and slamming the office door.

Matt blundered through the tack-room past

Kirstie. Then, without saying another word, he strode out of the corral.

Brad wouldn't harm Little Vixen! Kirstie insisted to herself. No one in their right mind would set fire to a barn and leave a champion reining horse and four other beautiful horses to die!

'I know what folks are sayin',' Brad told Kirstie.

His remark came out of the blue, after they'd worked with Little Vixen on her 360 degree turns. All was quiet in the corral. Behind them, the charred remains of the barn stood as a dull reminder in the gathering dusk.

'Huh?' Kirstie played dumb as she rubbed down the horse's sweating shoulders and back.

'It ain't true,' he said point blank.

'Hey, listen, I don't know . . .'

'Sure you do. You know they're pointing the finger at me for this.' Brad jerked his thumb towards the barn. 'Most likely you agree with them too.'

She took a brush and worked with long, determined strokes, saying nothing.

'But I'm tellin' you, Kirstie: no way did I start that fire!'

Litte Vixen jerked her head towards him. She blew through her nose and restlessly swished her tail.

'Easy, girl!' Kirstie tried to steady her and close her own ears to Brad. She felt like she was on a rack, being stretched.

'OK, then. Go ahead, believe your brother!' Giving a disappointed sigh, Brad turned to walk away.

Vixen snickered after him.

Kirstie looked at the dejected set of his shoulders. Brad was shaking his head, acknowledging that he'd lost the argument before it had really begun.

'Brad!' She called him back.

He turned, nursing the injured shoulder with his good arm, his face in shadow under the brim of his hat.

So Kirstie untied Little Vixen and walked her across the corral after her owner. The horse's hooves thudded quietly; her tail swished as she eagerly followed Brad.

They caught him up at the far side of the corral, where the entrance to the barn used to be. The smell of burnt wood filled their nostrils.

Kirstie looked hard at Brad, trying to read behind the guarded expression. How did you know when a person was sincere? How did you untangle the truth from the lies?

'I know how it looks,' he admitted quietly. 'And, if you really wanna know, I don't honestly blame Matt for thinkin' the way he does.'

She didn't contradict or smooth away the problem. No; she realised Brad genuinely wanted to tell it like it was.

'My way of actin' don't go down real good with some folks. It gets under their skin. But after all this time I'm stuck with it, I guess.'

She nodded. Yeah, she understood what he was saying. We were all landed with an image which we weren't totally in control of. It just so happened that Brad's was loud and brash.

'And, to tell you God's honest truth, I did come here to Half-Moon Ranch with half an idea in my head that I could charm the pants off your mom and work my way into some nice, cosy, rent-free situation.'

Kirstie bit her lip and frowned.

'That was before I met her,' Brad said quickly. 'I thought maybe I could cut and run from the

Double L and find a corner here where I could carry on trainin' Vixen, maybe in return for givin' more lessons to the guests. What was wrong with that?'

'Nothing,' she mumbled. If that was the whole truth. 'But you didn't need to use your charm on Mom. A straight business deal would've been enough.'

Brad gave a short, self-deprecating laugh. 'Yeah. She's a great lady.'

Kirstie's frown deepened. 'She likes you too.'

'It kinda scuppers my half-baked idea about movin' in on her, though. What I'm sayin' is, no way did I predict havin' ... feelings!' Embarrassed, Brad turned to look at the burnt out ruins of the barn. 'And that was the mess I'd got myself into *before* this happened!'

'Total mess,' she agreed.

'So what do I do now?' He appealed to her with a helpless shrug. 'Do I just pack my bags and get the heck out of here?'

'And make it look like you're running away? Yeah, great!'

'So I stick around and wait for the insurance people to pin this on me?' Brad made it clear that this option didn't appeal. 'That's what they'll try to do as soon as Matt tells them his side of the story.'

'But they'd still need evidence of arson,' Kirstie pointed out. 'Which, if you're telling me the truth, they're not gonna find!'

Brad's gaze flickered away for an instant, then grew steady again. 'That's right,' he insisted.

'So, stay. Wait for the accident verdict.' Slowly siding with Brad, she began to feel uncomfortably guilty about what she'd say to Matt next time their paths crossed. 'What do you have to lose?'

He still wasn't convinced. 'If I cut loose, that proves my guilt? If I stick around, I take more abuse from your brother? He poisons the minds of the others, your mom included. Gee, that's a great prospect!'

'Stay!' Kirstie insisted in a level, firm voice. Then she threw out a challenge which she knew Brad was honour bound to accept.

'Sure, it'll take guts. But if you run away from this now, the whole world has you down forever as a crazy, cold-hearted guy who tried to kill his own horse!'

7

'There are a hundred reasons why a fire might start,' Debra Chaney explained to Lisa and Kirstie on the Friday afternoon.

The girls had travelled home from school together, since Lisa was once more planning to spend the weekend with her grandfather at Lone Elm. She'd stopped off at the ranch with Kirstie especially to see what progress the insurance company's loss adjuster was making with her investigations into the cause of the barn fire.

Ms Chaney was a thin woman in her thirties,

practically dressed in jeans and lightweight fleece jacket. Her reddish-brown hair was cut short, but any masculine effect was softened by her small, dark features and heavy use of mascara.

'When I visit a site, I don't get involved on the personal level,' she continued, in response to Lisa's eager questions. 'My brief is purely scientific. If you like, I'm a kind of forensic expert looking for clues which the lab can then process.'

As she talked and Sandy Scott stood quietly to one side, Kirstie and Lisa helped her to rope off the site of the fire. 'I guess this really is like looking for a needle in a haystack!' Lisa quipped.

'Except there's nothing left of the haystack,' Kirstie pointed out.

Ms Chaney set about marking out the roped-off area into smaller sections, treading carefully through the charred beams so as to disturb them as little as possible. Nevertheless, her sturdy laced boots crunched through cinders and kicked up the ash, carrying it on the wind across the corral towards the house.

'So, when you say a hundred reasons, name me some.' Lisa caught the end of a nylon line strung out with orange markers which would intersect the barn floor diagonally from corner to corner.

'For instance, out of doors, you can have sunlight shining through a piece of broken glass which acts like a lens and intensifies the heat until the grass or the hay or the straw beneath begins to smoulder and then ignite.' Debra suggested one possibility.

'So you'd be looking for, say, the end of a broken bottle in the wreckage?' Lisa grasped the idea. 'What else?'

'If it's a barn where there are horses, you could think maybe the horse's metal hoof strikes an iron bolt on the door and causes a spark. The hay bales are so dry they'd go up in a flash.'

'But in which case there'd be no obvious clues.' Lisa thought this one through too.

'Right,' the investigator agreed. 'That's often the way with these things. It's easily possible that we never discover the cause, however hard we look.'

Pausing from the work to section off the area, Kirstie glanced up at her mom, who watched tensely, having been on tenterhooks all day, waiting for the woman to arrive. And now she stood, watching and hoping, knowing full well that Debra Chaney's verdict would affect the whole future of Half-Moon Ranch.

'What happens then?' Lisa wanted to know.

'I file a Cause Unknown report and the insurers then have to assume that the fire was an accident, bite the bullet and pay out for the owner to rebuild.' Satisfied with the preparations, Debra stepped outside the cordon and began to take a series of photographs of the extensive damage.

During the thirty minutes that this took, two of the day's trail-rides returned to the corral.

First came Ben on Hollywood Princess, the flashy white horse who liked to show off in front of the more down to earth sorrels and bays. Her prancing walk and the high-class carriage of her head marked her out, as well as the brilliant white sheen of her coat.

Behind her, the dude riders' horses seemed flatfooted and dull, strung out in a line that tailed a long way back along the side of the creek.

Before he reached the corral, Ben wheeled Hollywood Princess around and doubled back to encourage the tired guests. Meanwhile, Charlie's group headed down through the pine trees from

Coyote Trail, and the two sets of riders converged by the burnt out barn.

'Did she find anything?' Ben called to Sandy, nodding in the direction of Debra Chaney.

'Nothing yet.' Kirstie's mom had begun to pace up and down the corral. 'No news is good news, I guess.'

The assessor had finished with her camera and moved into the section of the wreckage where Kirstie had told her the fire had started. 'Here?' she asked, standing squarely in what had once been the central aisle of the barn.

From the edge of the site, Kirstie did her best to estimate the exact spot where Little Vixen's stall had stood. 'More to your left!' she called. '. . . OK, right there!'

Debora nodded and squatted down amongst the charred wood. She studied the area closely without touching anything at first.

'Gee, where would you begin?' Lisa shook her head in admiration at the methodical way the expert was going about her investigation.

Kirstie nodded but said nothing. Her own nerves were beginning to get the better of her; so much depended on this. It was a week ago exactly that her mom had said how she felt about the ranch; that it was pretty much perfect and they were the luckiest people alive to be in such a beautiful spot, living the way they wanted.

A week in which so many things had turned around and thrown up this big question mark over all their futures.

In the background, the two wranglers and their tired riders dismounted and unsaddled their horses. Kirstie noticed Matt emerge from the tack-room and busy himself in the corral. Hadley was there too, leading horses to water. There was no sign of Brad Martin.

By this time, Debra Chaney had reached forward and begun to poke about delicately amongst the ashes. Lifting one length of cindery wood, she disturbed several others, so that the fragile pile collapsed with a dry rustle. 'You're sure this is the spot where the fire began?' she re-checked with Kirstie.

'Yeah, because I saw it flare up behind Little Vixen. I reckon it started back in the corner of the barn, under that heap of metal sheets.' She pointed again to the chaotic pile of roofing material that had collapsed in on itself when the supporting beam had burned through. 'D'you want me to come across and help?'

'No. You stay right there.' Debra stepped gingerly over the unstable corrugated sheets and began to pull at a corner of one. She worked on, ignoring the bunch of onlookers who had drifted out of the corral, intent on examining every inch of the ground which Kirstie had identified.

'So far, so good,' Lisa whispered to Kirstie, going on the no-news-is-good-news principle.

They watched as Debra removed six foot long and three foot wide sheets of scorched metal, gradually gaining access to what lay beneath.

After ten minutes, she had cleared away the roof and had once more pulled out her camera to take close-up shots of the blackened ground.

And by now, there was a feeling passing like electricity between the onlookers that the investigator had reached the core of the matter. Everyone was quiet, their attention fixed on the flash of the camera. Then, when Debra stopped and put it to one side, crouching right down towards the ground and sticking in a small flag marker, the whole audience seemed to hold its breath.

Kirstie watched Debra stoop and at the same time feel inside her jacket pocket for a small plastic envelope and a pair of tweezers. The envelope was obviously for any relevant sample to be sealed in and taken to the lab.

The assessor tilted her head to peer underneath a burnt metal door hinge leaning against a charred plank. There was a gap of a couple of inches which she reached into with the tweezers. Then she picked up a small white object and pulled it out, popping it quickly into the specimen envelope and standing up straight.

The movement set the crowd buzzing.

'What did she find?'

'Did you see what it was?'

'Hush, she's coming over to Sandy. Listen!'

'Oh, gee!' Lisa breathed out heavily. 'This could be bad!' She drew Kirstie across the corral to join her mom and Debra Chaney.

'Mrs Scott, I have found something that might link up with the fire,' Debra said quietly, almost with regret. 'It's enough to send to the lab in any case.'

Sandy's frown was deep. 'Does it mean this wasn't an accident?'

'Not necessarily. It could still be pure carelessness. But I'm afraid it might raise a few suspicions that this could've been deliberate.'

Once more the onlookers buzzed and gossiped.

'I have to tell you, my company will probably want to bring the police in to investigate at this point,' the assessor went on. She seemed genuinely sorry to be the bearer of bad news. 'I guess you should prepare yourself. At the very least it's gonna mean quite a delay before you get a decision.'

'And at the worst?' Sandy asked quietly.

Ms Chaney paused, then gave it to her straight. 'At the very worst, the cops might want to bring a prosecution for arson.'

'Against me?' Sandy's voice was fainter than ever.

There was another short delay as Debra held up the clear envelope to display its contents. She made plain the likely outcome. 'If they arrest anyone, it will most likely be the person who smokes this particular brand of cigarette,' she concluded.

'You're gonna say you told me so.' Sandy had

spent a couple of hours alone, thinking through what Debra Chaney had discovered. Now she, Matt and Kirstie were walking together along the far side of Red Fox Meadow.

'Mom, believe me; I'd give plenty to have been proved wrong.' Far from crowing, Matt was subdued and sorry.

Sandy sighted and stopped to gaze at the horses grazing in the long evening shadows. Behind them, the mountains swept up to a golden horizon. 'Yeah. But I have to face facts. First, there ain't no one working on the ranch who smokes cigarettes except Brad. Second, I'm taking into account all you told me about the grudge he built up. Put the two together, and you gotta admit that makes him the prime suspect.'

'Why couldn't it be a guest?' Kirstie asked. Seeing her mom brought down so low was hard to take, so she sought other possible culprits.

'Because none of them smoke that brand either. I already checked.'

'So maybe it's a freak coincidence.' Kirstie tried again. 'Say Brad dipped into his pocket for something he needed when he was feeding Little

Vixen and pulled out the spent cigarette by mistake.'

It was Matt's turn to step in. 'Did you see the butt? It had burned halfway down, but it wasn't stubbed out. In other words, it had been thrown to the ground when it was still alight . . . In the barn . . . amongst the straw!'

'So how come it wasn't burned to a cinder?' Kirstie demanded.

Matt shrugged, then reached out over the white fence to stroke Cadillac's nose. The big white, aristocratic-looking gelding had sought him out as they strolled. 'I guess it survived the fire because it fell under something else that didn't burn right through. It's a stroke of luck for the insurance company.'

'And a disaster for us,' Sandy sighed.

'Anyway, Kirstie, how come you're so eager to speak out for Martin?' Matt wanted to know.

'His name's Brad,' she retorted. 'And I'm not speaking out for him. I'm only trying to be even handed.'

'Yeah, right!'

'Please, you two.' Turning wearily towards the house, Sandy began to walk away. 'For you to be fighting is just what I *don't* need!'

Matt glared at Kirstie and ran after his mom. 'We're sorry, OK? We won't argue any more. We just wanna help.'

She nodded. 'Thanks, Matt.'

'Tell us what we can do.'

'You can't do anything. None of us can. We just wait until the cops show up, which will probably be tomorrow. They ask us questions. We answer truthfully. What else is there?' Sounding exhausted, Sandy walked on slowly.

'I'll go ahead and make hot chocolate. You take it easy!' Anything, anything to try and please.

Kirstie let Matt make the attempt, knowing that it would take much more than a small treat to bring their mom back from despair. This was what happened when someone you trusted let you down. Brad had turned out not to be the man Sandy had thought and shown himself up as mean-minded, cruel and heartless.

Watching them go, Kirstie lagged behind, seeking comfort in the company of the horses close by. She hoped that five minutes spent with them in the quiet of the evening would soothe her before she had to face her mom wearing that same betrayed expression.

But she hadn't bargained on bumping into Brad Martin. She came across him tending to Little Vixen in the roped off area of the meadow closest to the corral. Wondering if Sandy and Matt had seen him too, Kirstie prepared to give Brad a wide berth.

'Hey!' he called as she tried to slip by. There was a forced bravado in his voice. 'How come Little Vixen here didn't get her workout this evening?'

Frowning, Kirstie hesitated then decided to speak her mind. 'Are you serious?'

'Excuse me?'

'I said, are you seriously saying we should go on here as if nothing happened?' Surely Brad knew about the assessor's recent discovery.

'What did I do?' He came across the grass towards her, swinging his leg over the fence and jumping down beside her. 'Listen, I mean it: why ain't nobody talking to me? Did I just commit a hanging offence without even knowing it?'

'The cigarette!' she exclaimed. She saw by his face that this was really the first he'd heard of it.

Come to think of it, Little Vixen and Brad hadn't been in either of the trail-riding groups who had returned while Debra Chaney had been doing her stuff. So she gave him the news and watched his handsome face set in bitter, frowning lines.

'Well, I guess that proves it,' he muttered, moving as if to pull out a pack of cigarettes from his back pocket, then thinking better of it. 'Yeah, your brother was right about me all along; I'm a no-good, lousy, low-down bum!'

Kirstie looked away helplessly.

'Didn't I tell you they'd pin it on me?'

'Yes, but you also said there wouldn't be any evidence of arson, and now look what they found!' *Explain this one to me!* she implored with a flash of her grey eyes.

'Look, maybe I did smoke a cigarette in the barn,' Brad conceded. 'But I'm careful. I always grind them down and heap dirt over them.'

'Not this one. And where were you to defend yourself this afternoon?' It seemed Brad was never there when the crucial events happened.

'Out riding,' he shrugged.

'With your arm in a sling?' she asked sceptically.

'Sure. I needed some thinking time. Anyways,

what difference does it make? Y'all made up your minds about me way back.'

'Not me.' Kirstie reminded him that only twenty four hours earlier she'd been willing him to stick around and prove the others wrong. 'And not Mom either.'

Brad clenched his teeth, then muttered through them. 'How about now? Do I still stand a chance of convincing Sandy that I'm innocent?'

This wasn't a question Kirstie could handle. 'You'd better ask her.'

Brad stared hard at her face. 'The answer's no, ain't it?'

Blushing, she turned away.

'Like I say, what difference does it make?' Giving it up as hopeless, Brad reached for his cigarettes a second time and drew out the pack. He found to his disgust that it was apparently empty and threw the whole thing to the ground. 'Yeah, guilty!' he muttered. 'Convicted without trial in this great democratic country. Well, God bless America!'

As he strode blindly away, Kirstie stooped to pick up the litter. Her head reeled; she didn't know what to think or do next. But as she went to slide the empty pack into her pocket, she heard a slight rattle from inside. Curiosity made her flip open the lid and tip out the contents.

Two half-smoked cigarettes fell into her palm; one end filtered, the other end of each one burnt out half way down its original length. She stared at them, puzzled. It seemed Brad had a habit of smoking half a cigarette and maybe overlooking it, going back to the ashtray too late and finding that it had gone out. In which case, he must slip it back into the packet to smoke later.

Kirstie looked up with Brad's name on her lips to call him back. But then she had second thoughts.

Instead, she pocketed the new evidence and headed across the footbridge to the scene of the fire.

Ought I to do this? she asked herself, glancing at the lights on in the house and twinkling from the windows of the cabins on the hill. *What am I hoping to prove?*

Hardly knowing the answer, she decided to go ahead. It involved ducking under the marker rope and stepping carefully over debris, making for the corner of the barn where she knew the fire had started. Then she had to locate the exact spot where Debra Chaney had picked up the cigarette. It was difficult in the dusk light, but eventually she found the small orange flag.

What had Brad said? That he always trod a spent cigarette butt into the ground and heaped dirt over it. Which must mean that if she looked closely in this small area, there would be a little pile of dirt and under it a squashed stub just as he'd described. She began to poke in the ashes with her fingertips, totally absorbed in the task.

. . . And if her theory was right, this might just mean that the half-smoked cigarette which was on its way to the lab right this minute had in fact slipped harmlessly out of the packet on to the floor as Brad took out a fresh one to light. Which would be a way of proving his innocence and starting over with their investigations.

It would mean something else had started the fire. Brad wouldn't be charged. Her mom could start believing in him all over again.

8

'Nice try, Kirstie!' Matt had listened to her new theory without relaxing the stiff frown he'd been wearing since the start. He'd accepted the grubby, squashed cigarette stub which she'd handed to him and reined back his comments until she'd told him and Sandy the whole story.

'But I found that stub twelve inches away from the marker!' she protested. 'It was half buried in the dirt. So Brad was obviously telling me the truth.'

'No, it doesn't necessarily follow.' Her brother

was infuriatingly calm as he argued back. Her mom sat at the kitchen table, her face in shadow, a halo of yellow light from the lamp behind her lighting up her long, fair hair. 'You could figure it this way,' Matt continued. 'Brad and I have the fight about payment. He storms off into the barn and smokes a cigarette to steady his nerve. Then he grinds it out underfoot. He kicks dirt over it so no one notices he's been such a darn fool as to light up close to the stack of hay.

'Then this puts another idea into his head. He gets to thinking, "Yeah it would be real easy to set fire to this place." And if he went ahead and burned down the barn, that would serve us right as far as he's concerned. Also, the fire would destroy the horses, and guess what, along would come 10,000 dollars for the accidental death of Little Vixen . . .'

'No, I just won't believe that!' Kirstie knew that Matt hadn't seen Brad's face when she broke the news about the so-called evidence against him. He'd been shocked and horrified, then angry. And she'd been convinced at that moment that he would never have risked his horse's life; not for a *million* dollars.

'That's because you let your heart rule your head,' Matt insisted. 'But what's staring us in the face is that after Brad has smoked the first cigarette, he gets the idea to pay us back and solve his own problems, both at the same time. So he lights up again and tosses the burning cigarette into the hay close to Vixen's stall. He makes his exit through the far end of the barn and slips away without anyone seeing him.

'Then it's only because you hear the horses kicking up a fuss in the barn and go in there and discover the fire in time for us to bring them out that they're not all killed!'

Kirstie felt her resistance to Matt's argument slip as he went forcefully on. Still their mom was saying nothing but thinking plenty. Probably her own heart was on Kirstie and Brad's side, but her head went along with Matt.

It was just as Matt had finished making his case, that they heard Brad's pick-up kick into life. The sound made Sandy jerk to her feet, then just as suddenly sit back down.

'What the . . .' Matt strode to the porch and looked out, followed quickly by Kirstie.

'He's leaving!' she gasped.

The headlights were on, raking across the yard as Brad turned the trailer around. From inside the box they could hear a horse whinny and stamp.

'Little Vixen's going with him!' Kirstie jumped down the step and began to run towards the pick-up. 'Brad, stop! Don't go!'

Catching sight of her in the headlights, he leaned out of the window, his face blank and shadowy. 'Give me one good reason why not.'

'Stay. Tell the truth about what happened.' She reached out to grab the door handle, as if this would keep him at Half-Moon Ranch to prove his innocence.

'Who'd listen?' he shot back through clenched teeth. He noticed Sandy standing under the porch light, framed by the doorway and making no attempt to join in with Kirstie's argument.

And by this time, Matt had arrived. 'Go ahead!' he mocked. 'Drive anywhere you like. But don't think you're gonna get away with this!'

'Says who?' Brad argued grimly. Holding the steering wheel with his good arm, he revved the engine and inched towards the gate.

'The cops will pick you up, no problem!' Matt

yelled after him. 'You and your fancy trailer and that champion reining horse!'

'Yeah, let them try.' Gathering speed, he forced Kirstie to let go of the handle.

She had to step quickly back, catching a glimpse of Little Vixen's white head through the trailer window as Brad drove on. The sight of the horse's rolling eyes, the sound of her frightened, stamping hooves sent Kirstie running to catch up once more with the driver in his cab.

'Where are you going? What'll you do?' she gasped.

But Brad gripped the wheel and steered one-handed, refusing to answer. 'Stand back!' he warned. 'I don't want no one to get hurt!'

'Don't . . . please!' Again she lost contact with the pick-up, felt the trailer slide by, its gleaming white shape towering over her as it passed. There was another momentary glimpse of Vixen's head, then the red tail lights as Brad took the trailer out on to the track.

'Mom, stop him!' Kirstie turned to appeal to Sandy, still a shadowy figure on the porch.

But her mother didn't move, and Matt was already swinging the wide gate shut after the trailer, muttering that he would call the cops and they would pick Martin up before he hit Route 3 into town.

Kirstie saw the red lights wink and then disappear round the first bend on the dirt road through the forest. 'He's crazy!' she whispered, feeling her heart sink.

'Mad and bad,' Matt confirmed.

The gate clicked, the yard fell silent. Beyond Elk Rock, a pale moon rose. A coyote called. Out in Red Fox Meadow, the horses huddled together for safety, whinnying after Little Vixen to warn her there was danger lurking in the forest. The coyote howled a second time and was answered by two more wild yips from high in the mountains.

Shivering, Kirstie turned and went back into the house.

To everyone's surprise, it proved harder for the cops to track down Brad Martin's trailer than they'd expected.

'One guy travelling along a forest road at night!' Matt said early next morning with evident disgust. 'Why do we pay Larry Francini good money if he can't even pick up a major criminal making his getaway one-handed in a vehicle with a maximum speed of thirty miles per hour?'

The San Luis sheriff had just called the ranch to say that as yet there had been no sighting of the runaway.

Warning Matt to calm down, Sandy told him and Kirstie that Sheriff Francini planned to drive over to the ranch to take down the details surrounding Brad's rapid exit. 'I guess he'll take a look at the barn while he's here,' she added. 'And there'll be more questions about that.'

Luckily for them, Saturday was the day when the week's routine wound down. Guests would be leaving, new ones arriving. But there would be no official trail-rides, and Ben, Charlie and Hadley would be able to take care of ferrying guests to and from Denver airport.

'Yeah well, when Francini finally makes it out to the scene of the crime, just make sure I get to talk to him,' Matt grumbled. 'If it's a motive for arson he's looking for, tell him I've got it all worked out for him and that all roads in this case lead to our missing celebrity, the Invisible Man!'

He strode out of the house to carry out chores while they waited, and Sandy made it plain to

Kirstie that she too needed to keep her mind occupied. 'I have to call Bill Almond and tell him not to bother showing up on Monday morning,' she said quietly. 'We can't drag an electrician all the way out here, then tell him there's no barn to work on after all.'

Remembering that this had been the reason why Charlie had driven into town for electric cable earlier that week, Kirstie let the remark slip by. She was immediately thrown off the subject by the ring of the phone, which she quickly picked up.

'Half-Moon Ranch,' she gabbled. Maybe this was hard news from the cops at last.

'Hey, Kirstie!' It was Lisa's voice, bright and breezy. After she'd lent a hand during Debra Chaney's visit, she'd been picked up by her grandpa and driven up with him to Lone Elm Trailer Park as planned. 'I guess things worked out for Brad after all?'

'Huh?' Kirstie walked with the phone out of her mom's hearing and spoke quietly to her friend. 'What makes you say that?'

'It looks like the cops didn't want to pin the barn thing on him. I just wanted to call and say

I'm glad for your mom it turned out that way.'

This wasn't making sense to Kirstie. 'Yeah, but hold on. What I'm asking is, what d'*you* know about it for chrissake?'

There was a pause before Lisa launched into a long-winded explanation. 'I'm using my head, putting two and two together...'

Yeah, and making five, Kirstie thought.

'I'm thinking, if the cops seriously want to interview Brad, no way would he be out and about. He'd be down the sheriff's office in San Luis by this time. But he can't be...'

'Why not?'

'Because I've just seen him drive his trailer up to Reception here at Lone Elm,' Lisa told her. 'Grandpa's given him a site. He's unloading Little Vixen right this minute!'

Straightaway Kirstie went looking for her mom. This was news that she couldn't keep to herself.

She found Sandy outside, walking around the rim of the burnt out barn, biting her lip in a thoughtful manner. As she approached, Kirstie played with various ways of phrasing this latest information, knowing the inevitable results.

First off, and most important, her mom would be upset all over again.

Second, Sandy would agonise and then decide that the news had to be passed on to the sheriff. And even though she must be by now pretty convinced that Brad had torched their barn, it would still be hard for her to break faith with him completely and send the cops up to Lennie's place to arrest him.

When it came to it, there was only one way to say it, and that was the simple, quick one. 'Brad's parked the trailer up at Lone Elm,' she told Sandy quietly. 'I guess he drove around the forest all night, then maybe ran out of gas or feed for Little Vixen. Anyhow, he decided to pull in at Lennie's place.'

Sandy closed her eyes and took a deep breath.

'What do we do now?' Kirstie asked.

'I'm working it out.' Opening her eyes and looking directly at Kirstie, she voiced her own troubled thoughts. 'I'm still not one hundred per cent convinced this is down to Brad.'

'Yeah well, you should've told him that,' Kirstie shot back without softening the message. 'He thinks *you* think he's guilty. That's why he gave up on us and drove off the way he did.'

'I know it,' Sandy confessed. Her eyes clouded over and she looked desperately sad. 'I just wasn't sure one way or the other.'

'And now?'

'I still don't know. But I feel I owe it to Brad, whatever Matt says, to keep on looking for other ways the fire could've started. That's what I was doing out here when you came to find me.'

Other causes still unknown. Kirstie frowned and recalled what Debra Chaney had told Lisa: that out of a hundred reasons behind a big fire, many often remained undetected. What instance had she given? The one about sparks created when a horse's shoe struck an iron bolt. That would be impossible for an assessor to pin down. Whereas, the one about the sun's rays striking a piece of glass would have been detectable. As would the remains of kerosene. And maybe, for instance, faulty electrical wiring . . .

'Jeez, Mom; Bill Almond!' Kirstie grabbed Sandy's arm and dragged her under the nylon rope which cordoned off the barn area.

'Kirstie, hold it. What do you mean, Bill Almond?'

117

'You're bringing him in to rewire the barn! Does that mean there was something wrong with the system we had?'

'Not wrong exactly. It's just old. Your grandpa first had electricity put into the barn thirty years back. I knew it needed updating as soon as we could afford it.' Sandy picked her way through the debris after Kirstie. 'Hey, wait a minute, I see what you're saying!'

Kirstie looked over her shoulder and nodded. 'What happens when an old wire or a socket gets worn out?'

'The plastic coating around the metal flex breaks, and if two pieces of bare flex make contact, it creates a spark!'

Nodding, she headed for the vital spot. 'The fire started here. There was a wall here, at the back of Little Vixen's stall.' Carefully she picked her way across a stack of roofing sheets and found the remains of a wooden partition. 'Where was the nearest electric socket?' she asked Sandy.

Her mom considered the answer. 'There was a meal bin standing here by the main post, and a wire running along the bottom of the partition to a socket right here.' Stooping to shift some

118

burned planks, Sandy put her hand on a length of wire which trailed along the ground. She followed it to what had once been one of the old plugs and sockets due for replacement.

Hidden under the planks and overlooked by an over-eager investigator, the socket on the remains of the partition was part-melted and covered in ash. But its small, square shape was still recognisable.

They could make out the black plastic box and the metal slots which had received the two-pronged plug. But the plug itself had detached from the socket, perhaps shoved out or loosened by Little Vixen in her effort to get at meal inside the bin. The movement could have dislodged a wire inside the old socket; metal could have made contact with metal. The entire plastic socket could simply have melted and burst into flames!

9

The thirty minutes between Sandy and Kirstie's discovery and Sheriff Larry Francini's arrival at the ranch were filled with frantic discussion.

Kirstie's mom had immediately drawn Matt in and insisted that the melted socket could throw new light on the whole situation.

Grudgingly he'd admitted that it might indeed alter the way the police would react.

'Except that we passed a safety inspection only last fall,' he'd reminded them. 'We have to renew our certificate every year for the insurance to stay valid.'

'Well, at least we're covered,' Sandy had pointed out. 'And it may have been a freak accident; nothing to do with the age of the wiring.'

'We think maybe Little Vixen kicked at the meal bin through the partition,' Kirstie had explained. 'And the meal bin caused a problem with the socket.'

'Mom, you've gotta be the one to pass this on to Brad!' Kirstie insisted as the three of them waited in the yard for the sheriff. They could see the car winding its way down through the trees, about half a mile from the ranch.

'Wait until we've spoken with Larry,' Sandy insisted. 'We wouldn't want to raise Brad's hopes without good reason.'

So they went through the whole thing again with the upholder of the law in San Luis County, from the original discovery of the half-burned cigarette by Debra Chaney, to Kirstie's unearthing of the buried second stub-end, through to this morning's investigation of what remained of the barn's electrical system.

Larry stood and listened, tilting his stetson to

the back of his bald head and folding his sturdy arms across his chest. Even when Kirstie butted in to her mom's account with her theory about the meal bin knocking against the socket, the sheriff's expression remained unchanged.

'Well?' Kirstie demanded. 'Does that mean you call off the search for Brad?'

'Not so fast,' Larry warned. 'The way I heard it from Matt last night, Brad Martin was pure evil. The guy was capable of mass murder, according to you.'

'I guess I overreacted,' Matt confessed. 'We're under a lot of pressure here, Larry. And the notion that the guy might have been willing to sacrifice those horses for the sake of a lousy insurace pay-out was driving me nuts!'

'To be fair, we did get the same message from the insurance company,' the sheriff pointed out in his slow, measured way. 'Their first response when they contacted me last night was that this looked like a case of arson. They're the ones who wanted me to move in and take a look.'

'But now it's all different!' Kirstie spread her hands in a gesture of impatience. 'It's not fair for you to push this on to Brad. You have to call off your search!'

'Whoa!' Larry Francini uncrossed his arms and hitched his thumbs through the loops of his trouser belt. 'There are a few things still bothering me. The main one being, if Martin's suddenly all squeaky clean, what's he doing running off the moment someone mentions the word "cop"?'

'Yeah,' Matt murmured, making it clear that his own anti-Brad reaction hadn't totally faded.

'Because he knew no one was gonna believe him!' Kirstie grew more exasperated.

Francini twitched his heavy black moustache, then sniffed. 'Not a very smart move in my opinion. In fact, it's still a mite suspicious, so I ain't gonna abandon the search right now.'

Kirstie sighed and looked down. This was going less well than she'd hoped.

The sheriff picked up her disappointment. 'But I'll tell you what I'll do,' he promised. 'I'll call the insurance company and tell them to send their Ms Chaney back out here to take a second look. Meanwhile, though, I'm passing the word around the ranches hereabouts that if anyone spots a pick-up pulling a white trailer, they're to call me right away.'

There was a silence as Larry brought the brim of his white hat forward on to his forehead and prepared to climb back into his car.

Kirstie looked anxiously at her mom, guessing what was coming next.

'Larry!' Sandy stepped forward as he opened the car door. Then she hesitated and her face coloured up. '. . . About Brad's trailer. There's no need to contact the ranches and put out an alert.'

Sheriff Francini nodded and waited. His expression said that nothing in life surprised him and that everything fell into place at last as long as you were prepared to be patient.

By now Kirstie was wishing that Lisa had never called and passed on the fugitive's whereabouts. Then she, Kirstie, wouldn't have been able to put her mom in this terrible spot, between a rock and a hard place.

'We heard where Brad is,' Sandy confessed. 'He showed up an hour since at Lennie Goodman's place. If you drive up there now, I'm pretty certain that's where you'll find him.'

'What's Brad gonna do when he sees that cop car drive through the gates of Lone Elm?' It was Sandy's turn to be stricken by guilt. 'He'll know somebody turned him in, and before too long he'll work out it was me!'

'So we call Lennie and get him to bring Brad to the phone.' Kirstie thought fast. 'So long as we can explain about the melted socket, Brad will realise that his best plan is to stay right where he is and talk to Larry, get his story straight and hope that Debra Chaney is willing to change her opinion about what started the fire.'

Her mom grasped at this idea and ran into the house. She punched the Lone Elm digits on to the key pad and waited for the phone to ring.

'No reply,' she reported to Matt and Kirstie. Slamming down the receiver, she strode restlessly out on to the porch.

'Why don't we drive up there?' Matt suggested, thinking of the ten mile journey. 'If we take a couple of back trails, I reckon we could make it at about the same time as Larry.'

Once more, Sandy seized the suggestion. 'Jump in the back, Kirstie!' she yelled, as Matt ran for the car keys and she slid into the front passenger seat.

'No, listen, Mom! I'm gonna saddle up Lucky and bushwhack along Bear Hunt Overlook. That route cuts the distance by as much as two thirds, so there's a chance I'll get there faster than any car!'

With no time to stop and consider, her mom agreed. 'Good thinking. We'll meet you up at the trailer park. But take care, OK?'

Matt jumped in the car and started the engine, setting off across the yard as Kirstie promised that she wouldn't try anything dangerous.

'Lucky knows the territory,' she assured Sandy. 'Don't worry about me. Just think about getting there fast and filling Brad in on the new developments!'

So Sandy settled in for the twisting dirt-road ride along National Forest tracks, while Kirstie ran for Lucky's saddle. Within a couple of minutes, she'd slung the heavy equipment over a rail in the corral, raced out to bring her palomino in from the meadow, saddled and bridled him and was ready to set off.

'This has to be fast,' she told Lucky, setting him

off at a trot which pretty soon became a lope.

Her urgency seemed to transmit to him. He went willingly at the steep slope out of the valley, ignoring the trails and cutting between the fresh green aspen trees with their slim, silvery trunks, up into the bleaker landscape of the lodgepole pines.

'Good boy!' Kirstie breathed, crouching low in the saddle, weight forward, knees flexed to absorb the shock of his galloping hooves. She felt the wind tug at her hair and balloon out the back of her shirt, heard it flap and the stirrup leathers creak as her horse made his way through Dead Man's Canyon, along Miners' Ridge towards the high, wild ridge of Bear Hunt Overlook.

Dodging low branches, swerving around trees, she judged their progress by the familiar landmarks. There was the tall, pointing finger of Monument Rock. Away to her left, the slope fell almost sheer to a bend in the river where the old miners had prospected for silver. Straight ahead, out of sight beyond the Overlook and still about a mile away was Red Eagle Lodge where Smiley Gilpin, the Forest Guard, hung out. Beyond that, another half mile across country was the entrance to Lone Elm.

'Go, Lucky!' Kirstie ducked another low branch and felt the sharp flick of pine needles in her face. Knowing that they were loping too fast for safety, still she was prepared to take the risk in order to reach Lone Elm before Sheriff Francini.

But as she and Lucky breasted the ridge and came within a stone's throw of the Forest Ranger's log cabin tucked away under a canopy of ponderosa pines on Timberline Trail, she spied Smiley Gilpin stepping down from his porch and waving to catch her attention.

'Hey, Kirstie! I got a message from your mom!'

Hearing this faint yell, she changed course and trotted Lucky up to the door. 'How come?' she asked the small, stocky ranger who waited in shirtsleeves, his thinning fair hair ruffled by the ceaseless wind. 'Mom and Matt are in the car, on their way to Lone Elm.'

'I know it,' Smiley replied. 'She called me on her cellphone. There's a hold-up on the road back by Jim Mullins's place. A logger's truck has jack-knifed on a bend. Nobody got hurt, but it looks like they won't be getting through for the next hour or so.'

'Right!' Kirstie drew breath. 'How about Larry Francini?'

Smiley shook his head. 'Nope, he didn't make it either. The accident happened before he arrived. He's dealing with it right now, bringing in a caterpillar truck from a cow station to shift the logs from the road.'

'Good.' Unable to hide her relief, Kirstie knew she could ease up a little. There was no doubt about it now; she and Lucky were going to be the first to reach Lone Elm and explain the new situation to Brad. It would all depend on how easily she could convince him that he was no longer the prime suspect in a case which was rapidly collapsing around the insurance assessor's ears.

Thanking Smiley, she set out on the last leg of the journey, crossing Timberline Trail then plunging down into the more sheltered valley beyond.

This time her landmark was a solitary ancient tree at the entrance to Lennie Goodman's trailer park. She allowed Lucky's pace to slacken, feeling him tire after his hell-for-leather lope. 'Good boy!' she whispered as he went willingly on, beyond the boundary of the National Forest into a greener, more open landscape.

The palomino sensed that they'd reached their destination and picked up speed once again along the level track that led under the arched wooden entrance. A sign to visitors welcomed them to the trailer park and invited them to check in at the desk.

Saturday morning was a busy time. Kirstie saw three giant Recreational Vehicles parked up

outside Lennie's office and several small knots of vacationers waiting in line to go into the office. Quickly checking that Brad wasn't amongst them, Kirstie stayed in the saddle and trotted by. She needed to find Brad's site and talk to him double-quick.

'Hey, Kirstie!' Lisa came cycling down a wide dirt track between a grove of aspens. Her red hair caught the sunlight; her white T-shirt and blue shorts looked cool and summery.

'Yeah, hey Lisa! Listen, this isn't a social visit. I need to talk with Brad. Can you show me where Lennie put his trailer?'

'Sure.' Without asking questions, her friend tuned in to the seriousness of the situation. 'Follow me.'

Lisa turned on the track and retraced her recent path between the shimmering trees. 'I just came by there. Didn't spot Brad hanging out though.'

Regaining her breath after the hard ride, Kirstie let Lucky trot easily after the bicycle. They passed rows of RVs and trailers, each one set inside a level hedged area with a small concrete patio for barbecues.

'Brad asked to be as far away from other visitors as possible,' Lisa reported, working steadily to cope with the incline. 'Grandpa chose site number 45 because there's good grazing for Little Vixen out the back.'

'How did Brad seem?' Kirstie asked anxiously.

'I don't know. I didn't talk with him,' Lisa admitted, eventually abandoning her bike at a corner of the track and turning on foot into the hidden plot of land where Brad's unmistakeable white and silver trailer stood gleaming in the sun. The ramp was lowered and, further forward, the door leading into Brad's sleeping compartment was open, as if the occupant must be somewhere close by.

So Kirstie dismounted and quickly glanced inside the horse-box. 'Empty,' she reported to Lisa, who immediately went around the back of the plot to explore the green culvert.

'If Little Vixen's not here, it means Brad took her out for a ride,' she called back.

'That can't be right,' Kirstie murmured. Why would Brad have ridden out and left the door open?

Tethering Lucky, she stepped up and peered inside the trailer.

There was a sleeping-bag unrolled on the bunk, a pot of coffee left to go cold on the miniature stove, and other signs that Brad had departed in a hurry.

What's he playing at? The disorder bothered Kirstie. Spruce-looking Brad hadn't struck her as the sort who would leave his expensive boots kicking around on the floor or, for that matter, the door open for folks to walk in.

'The horse ain't there,' Lisa reported back, climbing into the trailer to join Kirstie. 'But I did see recent tracks heading up Tigawon Springs Trail.'

Kirstie frowned and nodded. 'Something weird is happening here,' she muttered, her heart fluttering as she picked up a pack of cigarettes from the tiny table next to the cooker. Underneath was what looked like a brief note scribbled on a fragment of yellow paper.

'What's it say?' Lisa asked in a breathless voice.

It was a few seconds before Kirstie could make out the scrappy handwriting. And when she did, the fluttering of her heart turned into a sudden, plummeting thump.

' "Sell the trailer to pay my debts to Rex Evans," ' she read out loud in a quivering voice, discovering that the letters had begun to float before her eyes. ' "When you find Little Vixen, take her to Half-Moon Ranch. Ask Kirstie to look after her real good. Tell Sandy not to be sad." Signed, Brad Martin.'

10

'Typical guy!' Lisa cried after she'd worked through what Brad's note implied. 'He can't face up to his problems, so what does he do? He runs out on everyone, including his precious horse!'

But Kirstie shook her head. 'I reckon it's worse than that.'

'How do you mean, worse?' Jumping down from the trailer, Lisa stared up the Tigawon Springs Trail, as if Brad might possibly have changed his mind, and he and his black-and-white paint would come jogging back towards Lone Elm.

'Brad didn't just run off, as you put it,' Kirstie insisted quietly. 'He saddled up Little Vixen and set out on his very last ride.'

'What're you saying?' Lisa gasped. She pointed to the yellow paper in Kirstie's trembling hand. 'That it's a suicide note?'

'What else?' There was only the one way to read it. 'Y'know, last time I talked with Brad, he was bitter and angry because no one believed in his version of what happened to the barn.'

'How about you? Did you think he was innocent?'

Kirstie sighed. 'Yeah. Eventually.' She recalled the earlier doubts she'd shared with Matt about the flashy cowboy who'd come courting her mom. 'But at that point, after Debra found the cigarette butt, it looked like nobody else believed him. That really got to him. The guy has a lot of pride, and it was taking a severe beating at Half-Moon Ranch, believe me.'

'So what do we do?' Lisa went into panic mode. She ran a few steps along the trail, then dashed back towards Kirstie.

'You go tell your grandpa there's an emergency. Say Brad and Vixen got lost, not the suicide stuff.

He can call Mom and Sheriff Francini, fill them in. Tell him I'm gonna ride right on out and pick up Little Vixen's trail.'

'Will you try and talk Brad out of whatever it is he's planning to do?'

Kirstie nodded.

Lisa watched uneasily as she swung into the saddle. 'Say, Kirstie, you don't think Brad's carrying a gun to . . . to . . . ?'

'Who knows?' Kirstie muttered. A shot to the head would be quick and easy. It might well be the method Brad would choose. 'Move it, Lisa. Find us some help fast!'

Saying this, she urged Lucky into a trot out of the trailer park, quickly picking up the only set of recent hoofprints leading along the trail to Tigawon Springs. The extended hind shoes – the speciality reserved for professional reining horses – were the telltale sign that Lisa had hit upon the right exit route for the desperate man.

It was a route Kirstie hardly knew; well beyond the limits of the trail-rides followed by guests at Half-Moon Ranch. But at least she found it an easy track to follow, since the dense, dark forest of ponderosa pines to either side cut out the possibility of bushwhacking across country. The scaly tree bark gave off a strong, sweet smell of resin, and the fallen needles created a pale brown carpet on top of the soft, peaty soil.

There was Little Vixen's track, sunk deep into the dark earth, which had been kicked up by her galloping heels. It was unswerving and unbroken, heading out of the overhead trees, then it bent to the right up a steep open slope, cutting out a hairpin bend on the official trail.

As Kirstie reined Lucky sideways to follow Little Vixen's prints, she felt him hesitate, change his leading leg and lean into the slope. Then he went like the wind again, maybe sensing the fact that they were closing the gap between them and the horse and rider ahead.

Up here on the exposed mountainside, Kirstie felt the wind cut more keenly through her lightweight shirt and the T-shirt beneath. They were well above 12,000 feet, the air was thin, the sky a clear blue.

Glancing up from the ground, she saw the white peak of Tigawon Mountain; small sister to Eagle's Peak, but still rising clear of the snow line. Was that where Brad and Little Vixen were headed? Or had Brad chosen the fork in the trail which would lead to the Springs?

Kirstie reined Lucky back across a stretch of rocky ground, unable for a time to follow the prints. The palomino pranced and fought for his head, shaking his pale mane. 'Which way?' she whispered.

Along the narrowing, looming path leading between sheer cliffs to Tigawon Springs? It was a lonely spot where winter snow melt would still be crashing over the rocks from ledge to ledge, tumbling down dizzy heights with enough force to take a reckless man and hurl him fifty feet to his death.

Or ever upwards, across the snow line into a silent white world of perpetual winter?

Kirstie puzzled for a few seconds over what Brad would choose.

But Lucky was in no doubt. He danced sideways in the direction of the mountain, giving a loud, high squeal, as if communicating with an invisible comrade up there in the snowy wastes.

So Kirstie went with the horse's instinct, giving Lucky his head and charging on up the mountain past patches of snow half melted into the black hollows and dripping in four foot long icicles from ledges overhead. Interspersed with the snow drifts were sunny spots bright blue with delicate columbines, then sunshine yellow, white and pink with other sub-alpine meadow flowers. All these colours flashed by as Lucky sped up the mountain.

'I only hope you're right!' Kirstie muttered to him. Since she'd lost Vixen's prints, she was having to rely on her horse's superior sense of hearing. For herself, she could hear nothing except the wind, nor see anything ahead but a vast white space where gnarled krumholz pines finally gave out and the snow took over.

Then, yes! She could see Vixen's trail again. The black-and-white paint had plunged across the snow line into drifts that must have come shoulder deep at times. Her rider had forced her on, tracking more lightly across slopes where the wind had whipped the snow from the surface of the rocks and left them black and exposed. Lucky's whinny cracked the silence, his ears pricked.

What did he hear? Was there an answering call? Kirstie thought she caught a faint reply. Or was it imagined? If it was real, and Little Vixen was up here in the wilderness, where on earth did Brad think he was headed?

But that was it of course. The answer was 'Nowhere'. He was riding into the middle of an emptiness, a lonely figure cut off from the world. Maybe there above the snow line he might find the courage to take his own life. A place so remote that no one would ever find the body. Snow would fall gently on to the corpse, ice would encase it, avalanches bury it. It would never be discovered. No reasons offered, no misunderstandings. Simply the end.

Her heart squeezed with fear, Kirstie rode on.

She heard the heavy sigh of a horse across a waste of frozen water. She stood with Lucky at the edge of a small lake on a white plateau surrounded on three sides by steep slopes. This was where the trail had brought them – into a frozen basin, to a dead end.

Only the Bighorn sheep could pick their way out of the cul-de-sac, their sharp, neat prints zig-zagging out of the vast hollow on to the jagged ridge. Plumes of white cloud tore across the blue horizon, driven by the winds that howled down the slopes and whistled into hidden crevasses.

Kirstie looked and listened. Once more she heard the sigh, and this time a snort and the light jangle of a bridle.

'Smart boy!' she breathed in Lucky's ear, slipping from the saddle and tying him to the stump of a rotting tree. She resisted the urge to call out Brad's name, and instead crunched her way carefully around the rim of the lake, expecting to find him and Little Vixen in every one of the narrow ravines she passed.

But each time she was disappointed and had to press on, her teeth chattering in the sub-zero temperatures, her heart almost stopping with fear at what she might discover.

She'd covered half the perimeter of the small lake, had decided to yell for Brad to show himself since he'd probably already worked out that someone was on his trail.

She would say, 'It's me, Kirstie. Listen, Brad, don't do anything stupid. I need to talk!'

He would abandon the plan to kill himself. Everything would work out fine.

And yet, every second, as her feet crunched

142

through the frozen snow, she expected to hear the sharp click of a trigger cocked for action, the blast of a gunshot reverberate around this desolate place.

'Little Vixen!' Surprise brought the horse's name to her lips as she peered behind the next tower of bare, vertical rock. She stood on a narrow, icy ledge, her back to the lake, still picking her way around the perimeter.

The horse stood fully saddled, her breath rising in white clouds of steam, her mane stiff with ice. She wasn't tethered; simply standing, head down, waiting for Kirstie to arrive.

'Where's Brad?' Thinking that she'd never seen anything so forlorn as the riderless horse, Kirstie moved closer.

Vixen stamped and tossed her head.

'Did he leave you all alone?' she murmured, remembering the chilling finality of the note that had signed Little Vixen over into her care. 'Where did he go?' she asked, afraid that it was too late.

It was a fear that made her turn quickly on the ledge and almost lose her footing. She had to be sure that the surface of the ice on the lake wasn't cracked and broken, that no crazy person had already flung himself to his death.

Thank heavens, it was smooth and white and glistening.

'I'm up here,' a voice said.

Her head spun as she tilted it back and squinted against the sun into the blue sky.

She made out a silhouette gazing down at her from the tower of rock. Brad gave no reaction to her being there, as if it made no difference to what he planned to do.

'Don't ask,' he told her, raising his good arm to forbid her to speak. 'If I'm gonna do this, I'll do it without talkin' about it.'

'You rode all the way up here with your arm in a sling!' she chided. The words fell out of her mouth without engaging with her brain.

He shrugged. 'A guy can break his neck fallin' from a horse. It would be as good a way as any.'

'Don't talk like that, Brad. There's no need!'

'Listen, kid, I don't expect you to understand. This is the end of the line for me, that's all.' He stood on the twenty foot pinnacle. A leap into the blue would be all that it would take. No gun. No red blood on the snow. Simply a plunge through the ice and a cold, cold ending.

'There's just one thing,' Brad told Kirstie. 'You need to know, I wouldn't have harmed a hair on Little Vixen's head. Not for a million dollars. I love that horse.'

'I know it. But hear me out. Things have changed.' Kirstie's scrambled thoughts slowly came back together. But not fast enough to stop Brad from inching closer to the edge. 'No, don't!' she pleaded.

'I don't want much out of life,' he told her, staring beyond the ledge where she stood to the middle of the frozen lake. 'But I like to pay my debts. And I need respect.'

'I understand that! Honest! All I'm saying is, listen to what I have to say.'

'For what? So you can change my mind and get me sent to jail for something I didn't do?'

'No! So you can change their minds and stay *out* of jail. Don't give in. That's the easy way!' Kirstie shot the challenge at him, watching his tall figure sway forward, then steady itself. It had worked once. Maybe it would again.

Brad hesitated on the brink. 'I drove through the night thinking about this. Believe me, it ain't the easy way. But I ain't ready to spend years

146

locked up in a cell. There's worse things than dyin' and that's one!'

'So, don't!' At last, Kirstie gathered her courage to force herself to the point. *Please let him believe this!* she prayed silently. Nothing she'd ever said had been a matter of life and death the way this was now.

'Mom and me found out the fire was an accident,' she told Brad. 'We're not gonna let them arrest you. No way are you going to end up in jail!'

11

'And now we go over to Gladstone, New Jersey for an update on the situation at the US Equestrian Team Festival of Champions!' the excited TV presenter announced.

Kirstie, Matt and Sandy sat glued to the Sport channel, fingers crossed. They watched an aerial view of the stadium, then a swooping camera narrow down to a figure in the crowded commentary box. The broadcaster said he was almost ready to announce the result of the national reining championship.

'I can't take it!' Sandy hid her face.

A month had passed since Kirstie had persuaded Brad to come down from Tigawon Mountain with Little Vixen. He'd got Kirstie to screw up the note written on yellow paper and told her never to talk to her mom and brother about it.

'I won't,' she'd promised. 'And I'll swear Lisa to silence on pain of death!'

That would be a hard act for her friend. Silence wasn't Lisa's thing. But Kirstie knew that if she threatened to break friends forever, then there was a chance that Brad's secret would hold good.

'I swear!' Lisa had agreed, looking noble and resolved.

Sheriff Francini had arrived at Lone Elm with Matt and Sandy Scott, ready to go easy on Brad Martin after a second conversation with Sandy while the caterpillar truck had cleared the logs from the track. They'd heard about Brad's sudden disappearance via the cellphone and the sheriff had been as concerned as anyone to straighten out the whole darned mess as soon as possible.

So, after the jam had cleared and they'd reached the trailer park, they'd all set out on

Tigawon Springs Trail anxious to see that no harm came to either of the crazy people or the horses up there above the snow line.

'Kirstie doesn't even have a jacket!' Sandy had pointed out. 'She's gonna catch her death of cold!'

But before too long they'd met up with the bedraggled group; two exhausted horses, two taciturn people unwilling to go into detail about recent events.

'. . . So?' Matt had demanded after Kirstie was safely back in the ranch house and Brad was working things out with Sheriff Francini. 'What was with Brad and the mountain?'

Kirstie had turned to Sandy. 'Mom, do I have to explain? Can't it be between Brad and me?'

Her mom had looked at her long and hard. 'Is that what Brad wants?'

She'd nodded then sighed. 'Sorry.'

'That's OK. Matt, I guess we respect that, since everything worked out in the end.'

'Thanks to Lucky,' Kirstie had said. And then she'd refused to elaborate, except to say that her palomino had to be the smartest horse in the world.

'I thought that was Little Vixen,' Matt had teased.

But Kirstie had disagreed. 'Little Vixen's great at doing what you tell her; the sliding stops and the spins. She's a great athlete.

'But the thing about Lucky is that he figures stuff out for himself. Like, he knew how important it was to track down Vixen and Brad, so he just went right ahead and did it!'

'Brain versus brawn!' Sandy had laughed.

'Kinda. But they're both the greatest. I mean, really! There's not a single thing I would change about Lucky or Little Vixen even if I could!'

And Kirstie had continued to help Brad train Vixen at Half-Moon Ranch until his dislocated shoulder had healed. They'd worked on the horse's weak points, which Brad identified as swinging her quarters out too wide on the slow, weaving circles that led up to the fast spin. It had taken a lot of hard work to correct, but in the end they'd got where they wanted to be.

And Debra Chaney had come back to the scene of the fire and filed a revised report to her bosses saying that she was 99 per cent certain that the blaze had been down to a problem with the electrical socket behind Little Vixen's stall. All thought of criminal charges against Brad Martin had been dropped.

So Brad had finally got to concentrate on what he did best. His shoulder came good after two weeks. His way to Gladstone was clear.

Which was why Kirstie's family was now hanging on the commentator's every word.

'Neil Pitts on Miss Ellie finishes high in the competition ranking with a total of 222.5 points!' He talked fast to camera. 'Charlie Considine from Ocala, Florida is ahead with 225 points in all! But in the arena right now, riding like crazy to overtake that lead, is our last competitor, Brad Martin, on his beautiful black-and-white paint, Little Vixen! . . . Wow, look at that sliding stop to end the programme! That's gonna go a long way with the judges when it comes to awarding marks . . .'

'Oh, please win!' Kirstie whispered from her seat on the sofa.

Brad ended his routine and trotted a proud Vixen around the giant arena, watched by a crowd of 50,000.

'So who gets the 100,000 dollar first prize?

Who becomes this year's National Reining Champion?' The commentator's voice rose as the scores flashed up on the electronic board.

'That's a total of 224 points for Brad Martin on Little Vixen! . . . And would you believe it, Charlie Considine wins the championship for the second year running! Just listen to that crowd!'

'Jeez!' Kirstie slumped back.

'. . . And it puts Little Vixen well into the money with a second prize of 30,000 dollars!' the TV man told them.

'Oh, wow! 30,000 dollars!' Kirstie shot back out of her seat and watched Brad take off his hat to wave to the crowd. Little Vixen's head was up; she knew she'd done well. 'Hey, Mom, hey, Matt! We got second place!'

Brad would pay off his debt and still be able to rent a place he'd inspected just outside San Luis. He would be practically on their doorstep, yet far enough away to give both of them some breathing space, as Sandy had put it. No way was she rushing into any serious commitment right now.

'. . . Second place!' Kirstie went out to Red Fox Meadow and told Lucky the result of the competition.

The palomino listened with cocked head, then nodded wisely.

'Little Vixen swung out her quarters on one single turn,' she explained. 'So she lost a whole mark. We have to work on that when Brad gets home. Then next year at Gladstone, what do we do?'

Lucky blew down his nose and snickered.

'That's right; we make first place!' Kirstie laughed, giving the horse's neck a hearty slap. 'Brad earns enough prize money to buy his own place, and even Matt has to agree in the end that Brad is a good catch for our mom! That's what you just said, ain't it, Lucky? Yeah, you're a smart horse, Mr Palomino Wise-Guy!'

Another Hodder Children's book

HORSES OF HALF-MOON RANCH
Gunsmoke

Jenny Oldfield

A school group takes over the ranch for a
week. Kirstie befriends Lacey, a loner
with a natural talent for riding. Besotted
with her horse, a blue roan gelding called
Gunsmoke, Lacey breaks ranch rules and
rides off trail alone. When she fails to
return, Kirstie fears the worst; either Lacey
has had a terrible accident, or she's run
away – unaware that a heavy storm is
brewing . . .

HORSES OF HALF-MOON RANCH
Jenny Oldfield

All Hodder Children's books are available at your local bookshop, or can be ordered direct from the publisher. Just tick the titles you would like and complete the details below. Prices and availability are subject to change without prior notice.

Please enclose a cheque or postal order made payable to *Bookpoint Ltd*, and send to: Hodder Children's Books, 39 Milton Park, Abingdon, OXON OX14 4TD, UK.
Email Address: orders@bookpoint.co.uk

If you would prefer to pay by credit card, our call centre team would be delighted to take your order by telephone. Our direct line *01235 400414* (lines open 9.00 am–6.00 pm Monday to Saturday, 24 hour message answering service). Alternatively you can send a fax on *01235 400454*.

TITLE		FIRST NAME		SURNAME	

ADDRESS	

DAYTIME TEL:		POST CODE	

If you would prefer to pay by credit card, please complete:
Please debit my Visa/Access/Diner's Card/American Express (delete as applicable) card no:

Signature .... Expiry Date: ....

If you would NOT like to receive further information on our products please tick the box. ❏